I0669175

NAPALM PSALMS

LISA VASQUEZ   GAGE GREENWOOD   AJ BROWN

M ENNENBACH   ERIN BANKS   EZEKIEL KINCAID

EDITED BY
LISA LEE TONE

THE WAR INSIDE

CHARLES MANSON

"You know, a long time ago being crazy
meant something. Now everybody's crazy."

—Charles Manson

CHILD OF WAR
BY LISA VASQUEZ

There is a war, a war in me
It rips and tears, it bleeds and cries
It snaps, it snarls, it bends the knee
I try to smile, I build more lies
Fake it, make it, hyperbole
How can I breathe? I'm paralyzed!

All shit and piss
Remiss, dismiss
More ass to kiss
Immune to bliss
Stay tuned for this
A severed wrist

My reflection, shattered pieces
Staring back at strange new faces
Existence folds into creases
Origami truth replaces
All my memories, diseases
Wilted roses, broken vases

My Jack-in-the-box of trauma
The crank winds the demon tighter
Careful, don't you trigger momma
If you do, you'll have to fight her
Tethered by a Monster's dogma
Rage, burning brighter than fire

The weasel goes pop
All the pain won't stop
Slipping mask won't drop
The Devil's on top
The bruises won't stop
The beatings won't stop

The rope won't knot
. . .The blood won't clot
. . . . .The whispers won't stop
. . . . . .Please, make it all stop

Aileen Wuornos

"To me, this world is nothing but evil, and my own evil just happened to come out cuz of the circumstances of what I was doin"

—Aileen Wuornos

Autophagy
BY EZEKIEL KINCAID

Somewhere in Homophobic, Louisiana ...

No matter how many times his mother beat him, the homosexual demon still wouldn't leave fourteen-year-old Jeremiah Marsh. The thrashing happened on the night of his father's funeral, six days after he had passed away from renal failure. Over the years, the poor man had taken the brunt of the abuse, shielding Jeremiah from the wrath of his mother. Now, with him gone, Jeremiah sat helpless, like a lamb to the slaughter.

His father, Jonah Marsh, was a good man. A kind, patient man who would give you the shirt off his back and the last dollar in his wallet. Every kid would have loved to have a dad like him. Jeremiah looked up to him. He loved and adored him. He never knew the magnitude of the abuse or how far down the hyper-religious rabbit hole his mother trod.

But the revelation of the truth lay just around the corner.

He suspected his father stayed in the marriage to protect

him. Jonah was a wise and perceptive man. He knew. He knew the second he left how bad things would get.

And Jonah was right.

Jeremiah had known he was gay since he turned thirteen. It was a weird sensation at the start, being attracted to a male. He felt dirty and ashamed the first time the allure made itself known. It wasn't supposed to be this way, was it? Men liked women and women liked men. Anything else was an abomination. At least, that's what his mother, Millie Marsh, had preached.

It had been in seventh hour PE. The boys had finished a game of basketball and were changing in the locker room. Jeremiah glanced over at his best friend, Dalton Howard, who lifted his shirt just above his head. It wasn't that he noticed Dalton, it was how he felt when he did. *Attraction*. Like how a man would notice a woman.

His dad was the only person who knew about his secret. Jeremiah had told him about four months after the locker room experience.

"Are you ashamed of me, Dad?" Jeremiah had asked his father, looking up at him with sheepish eyes.

They sat on the edge of Jeremiah's bed.

Jonah shook his head. "No. Why would I be ashamed? You're my son. I love you."

Jeremiah's body relaxed, and he smiled. "Thanks, Dad."

Jonah rubbed his son's head. "Nothing will ever change my love for you. No matter what. Always remember that."

"Yes, sir," Jeremiah said with a nod. Then his face turned pale. "But, Dad?"

"What?"

"Please don't tell Momma. *Please*." His eyes watered, and a tear trickled down his cheek.

Jonah embraced his son. "I won't. We will not say a word

until you are ready. I won't tell your mother. I won't tell anyone."

Since then, Jeremiah did his best to hide it. But like all love and desire, it found its way to the forefront.

JUNE 13, 1999

THE SUMMER RAIN fell in heavy pitter-patters against the window in Jeremiah's room. He stood there numb, staring out into the gray haze of storm clouds and a watery canvas. Tears streamed down his face, and his body shook with the peals of thunder. In the darkness of his room, his voice escaped as a whisper into the night.

"Dad," he said. "Why did you have to leave me?"

The lightning flickered, illuminating his room like a camera flash. His lips quivered, and he released a heavy cry of mourning—the bell toll of grief birthed from a broken soul.

"You left me here ... alone ... with her. With her!" He backed away from the window and collapsed onto his bed. The lapels of his black suit scrunched towards his nose. As he took rapid breaths between his tears, he found himself lost in the aroma of the white carnation on his jacket. He had picked it from the flower arrangement on his father's coffin, and his aunt pinned it to the front of his coat.

Jeremiah curled his tiny body into a fetal position, inter-locking his fingers behind his head. *What am I gonna do? Oh God, what am I gonna do?* The only person he had trusted with the secret of his sexuality was dead. Fear ate away at his gut. It gripped him around the neck like a vice, choking all the courage out of his soul. If his mother found out, she would kill him. No, not just kill him. She would degrade, torture, and humiliate him. He recalled a conversation he overheard between his parents when he was twelve.

It had been late one night when Jeremiah was supposed to be in bed. He crept downstairs unnoticed and slipped into the kitchen to grab a snack. Jonah and Millie were seated in the living room watching television.

"Good Lord in heaven," Millie said. "Why do they have to shove all this homosexual stuff right in our face? This is revolting. No one wants to see two men kiss. I can't believe the state of this country. Next thing you know, they will be letting the faggots marry."

"Wow, Mille," Jonah said. "The Christ-like love you're showing is off the charts."

"Don't patronize me, Jonah. Who do these people think they are, trying to push their agenda on us God fearing folks."

"Agenda? Really? So they showed two gay guys kiss on television, and what? The homosexuals have a secret agenda to take over the world and make everyone gay? Good Lord, Millie."

"That's how it all starts. They push a little here and there. Letting their sin infiltrate the air waves," Millie said.

"I've had about enough," Jonah said. "I'm going to bed."

"Yeah, next thing you know, you'll be a liberal and voting Democrat. You need to wake up, Jonah."

"Nothing liberal about loving your neighbor and treating others like you want to be treated."

Jeremiah heard his father get up from the couch. He retreated to the doorway, ready to make a dash up the stairs. Before he made his exit, he waited to hear if his father would say anything else.

"These people ain't my neighbors, thank God," Millie said. "Besides, being gay is unbiblical. It's an abomination."

"You know what's more unbiblical?" Jonah asked. "Hate,

Millie. You'd probably turn on your own son if you found out he was gay."

THE CONVERSATION HAUNTED HIM. The words played in a loop over and over in Jeremiah's head as he lay there on the bed. He unlatched his fingers and ran his hands through his curly black hair. What was he supposed to do now? He hadn't told another soul. Not a teacher. Not a guidance counselor. None of his friends knew he was gay and neither did anyone in his youth group. It was a secret he kept buried in his bosom, and it ate him alive from the inside out.

The minutes ticked by, and the storm passed. Jeremiah looked over at the digital clock on his nightstand. The red numbers read 10:15 p.m. He rolled over and stood up off his bed. He undressed and tossed his suit on the chair next to his gaming desk. He clicked on the desk lamp and grabbed a copy of *Muscle and Fitness* magazine from the top drawer of the desk. His mom let him have the magazine because she thought he wanted to get into working out. And why not? He was five foot three, 120 pounds. If she knew the real reason he had the magazines, she would die.

He flipped through the pages and found a sexy man with a chiseled body, blond hair, and blue eyes. He laid down on his bed, holding the magazine with one hand and sliding down his briefs with the other. He started to work his manhood.

The bedroom door flew open.

A blanket of sheer, unadulterated panic draped over Jeremiah. He froze mid-stroke, his hand gripping his erection and his eyes the size of shot glasses. He had forgotten to lock his door amidst all the grief and memories.

The silhouette of Mollie Marsh in her pink sleeveless nightgown loomed in the doorway. Her hefty 250-pound frame stayed hidden in the shadows. The soft illumination from the lamp revealed a marshmallow-like face twisted in anger, with green eyes burning with rage.

"Jeremiah Nathan Marsh! You little pervert! What in the good God damn are you doing?" Millie thundered over to the bed, her monstrous footsteps shaking the floor.

Jeremiah couldn't move. It felt like his muscles had been replaced with stone and his skin with cement. He sat there with his mouth halfway open and his hand still wrapped around his cock.

Millie was on him before he could blink. She snatched the magazine from his hand. "Give me that pornography!" She stepped into the light to get a glimpse at the filth her son had put into his mind. "What is this crap?" She raised the magazine to her face.

Millie gasped as if she tried to suck all the air out of the room. Her entire overweight body quaked in anger. She flared her nostrils and bared her teeth in anger. A look of ardent disgust morphed her face into an unrecognizable creature. She grabbed the magazine in both hands and tore it down the middle.

"You!" She threw the two pieces at Jeremiah. "You disgusting, filthy ..." She clenched her fist in white-knuckle wrath. "Dirty fucking queer! What in God's holy name is wrong with you?"

The stone in Jeremiah's muscles turned to rubber, and the concrete around his skin melted like wax. He shook in terror at the sound of his mother's screams. "Ma, Ma, Ma, Momma ... I—"

"Not in my house! And how dare you! On the day of your father's funeral, I find out my son is a faggot! What do you think your dad would say, huh?" She stormed closer to Jeremiah, her brown, curly hair bouncing with each step. "We are gonna put an end to this right now!" She grabbed Jeremiah around the ankle.

"No, Momma! Stop!" He yanked his foot back towards his buttocks, bending his knee.

"Don't you pull away from me!" Millie crawled onto the bed and punched Jeremiah in the side of the leg.

"Owww! Stop, Momma!" Jeremiah's heart thudded away in his chest. Fear scorched through his veins, and tears rolled down his eyes.

"I'll stop when you quit being gay!" She grabbed Jeremiah by the hair and planted her weight fully on the bed. She gave his head a hearty yank.

Jeremiah's body lurched forward, and he latched on to her wrist with both hands. "Momma, stop! You're hurting me!"

Millie maneuvered her fat ass off the bed and stood to her feet, still gripping Jeremiah by the head. "I don't know how in the world this demon got into you, son. But we are gonna get it out!" She grabbed another handful of Jeremiah's hair and gave a violent tug.

Jeremiah slid off his bed and crashed onto the bedroom floor. His chin hit the ground, rattling his jaw and knocking out one of his front teeth. He scurried his knees up under his body as Millie pulled. He fought his way to both feet, pounding away on her arms with his fist. He spat out a mouthful of blood along with the tooth that had been jarred loose.

Millie watched the blood splatter to the floor and saw the white morsel sitting in the crimson puddle. "I bet your little faggot lover won't want you sucking his little prick with that ugly smile now."

Jeremiah wept and pleaded with his mother, his howls of anguish echoing through the entire house. Millie ignored her son's cries for mercy. She dragged him by his hair out of his room, into the hallway, and next to the staircase.

"Please, Momma! I won't do it again, I promise!" He twisted and torqued his body, trying to break her hold.

"You lie, demon!"

"It's me, Momma! I'm not a demon!" Jeremiah managed to break the hold of one of her hands.

Millie's forearm dangled in front of his face. In those brief moments, his survival instincts went into overdrive and he bit down on her like a rabid dog. She shrieked in pain, releasing the hold with her other hand. Millie made a fist, reached back, and punched her son in the side of the head.

The blow knocked Jeremiah loose from her arm and sent him tumbling down the stairs.

Jeremiah's world spun as he listened to his thudding body rumble all the way down. He lay on the bottom few steps, dazed and glassy eyed. The last thing he saw before he blacked out was his mother stampeding towards him, cursing the demons.

WHEN JEREMIAH AWOKE, he stared down at his naked crotch. He felt the cool metal of the steel chair against his buttocks. He looked to his left, then right. His ankles had been tied with ropes around the legs of the chair. When he tried to move his arms, he felt something dig into his wrist. He lifted his head, looking left and right again. His arms were tied behind the chair.

Then Jeremiah looked straight ahead.

There stood Millie. Her curly hair was in shambles, and her eyes twinkled with a hint of madness. She took heavy pants, her obese chest rising and falling with each breath under her pink nightgown. In her hand, she held the ivory-colored family Bible. Jeremiah remembered how massive it looked sitting on the coffee table. Now, swaying in his mother's hand, it seemed small in comparison to her meaty arm.

She had him tied up in the kitchen. The sink sat over to his left, and the hallway to the living room to his right.

Behind him was the table, and in front of him, peeking behind his mother, was the refrigerator.

Jeremiah licked his lips and spoke. "Momma, what are you doing?" His head pounded and his feet throbbed.

"It speaks," Millie said and raised the Bible.

Jeremiah saw a white blur, then the spine of the book smashed the bridge of his nose. A loud crack resounded across the room, and blood exploded from his nostrils.

"You demon of homosexuality! I command you in the name of Jesus to get out of my son!" Millie gripped the Good Book with both hands. She extended her arms, holding it in front of Jeremiah's face.

When his vision cleared, he saw the words HOLY BIBLE in gold font staring back at him, traces of his own blood smeared along the side. He hung his head and wept, his tears falling with the blood and dripping onto his crotch. His petite frame quaked with terror. Fear burrowed its way to a place deep inside him, creating a cold chill he felt all the way in his bone marrow.

His mother had transformed into an unrecognizable creature of terror. The smell of body odor and grease radiated from the sweat leaking from her pores.

"I ..." Jeremiah's teeth chattered. "I'm not ... a demon ... Momma."

She raised the Bible above her head, the fat on her flabby arms swaying with the movement. "Liar!" Millie brought the Word crashing down on the top of his skull.

Jeremiah squealed in pain as black and yellow spots ran across his vision.

"Shriek at the power of the Word, demon!" Millie tossed the Bible in Jeremiah's lap. She paced back and forth, wagging her finger at him. "You can't play games with me, Satan. I know who you are! What you're doing! And nope!" She paused, turned on her heels, and pointed her finger in his face. "You won't fool me!"

"Momma, please! Stop!" Jeremiah wheezed, then let out staccato moans.

Millie placed her hands on his knees and leaned into his face. Jeremiah caught a whiff of her breath. It reeked of sausage patties and orange Tang.

"Spread. Your. Legs!" Millie's eyebrows danced up and down with each word.

Jeremiah's eyes widened. "What?"

"You heard me, demon!"

He gave his head frantic shakes. "No. No, no, no, no."

"Fine!" Millie pushed with all her might, separating his knees from one another.

The top of the Bible fell against his penis, and the bottom slipped onto the seat of the chair.

"This demon is in deep, boy. It's infested all your body parts. You know why you wanna stick your pecker in ass? Huh! Do ya?"

"No, Momma!" Jeremiah's lips quivered as blood trickled from his nose. He closed his eyes and hung his head. His heart broke. How could his own mother do this to him? What did he ever do to her? He was her *son. Her son!* Mothers were supposed to protect their children, to show them unconditional love and understanding. Yet here she was beating him with a Bible and getting ready to do God knows what to his crotch.

The horror and stress collapsed onto Jeremiah. His bladder gave way, and his bowels released. He pissed all over the Holy Bible. The gas releasing from his rectum vibrated off the chair, and a brown flood of diarrhea followed.

Millie saw it all. She gnashed her teeth, flared her nostrils, and furrowed her brow. "You vile, filthy demon! How dare you desecrate God's Word!" She ripped the Bible from his lap and opened it down the middle. She slid her finger in, marking her place, then closed it. With her other hand, she reached out and grabbed Jeremiah by the penis, avoiding the liquid feces leaking out from under his testicles. "Time to go directly to the source!"

Jeremiah howled—part pain and part fear. "Momma, no! Stop! What are you doing? What are you doing, Momma? I'm scared! Please! Please don't, Momma! I'm sorry! I won't be gay! I promise! I won't be!"

"That's a goddamn lie, devil! That's all you do is lie! Lie! Lie! Lie! Lie! Lie!" She jerked his penis harder.

"Ow, Momma!" Jeremiah's high-pitched scream could have shattered glass.

Millie slid the Bible between his thighs and opened it. She let go of his penis and repositioned her hand. She grabbed his balls, paying no mind her fingers were getting covered in shit, and lifted all his manhood up. She set it in the center of the Bible. "In the name of Jesus, come out!"

Millie slammed the Bible shut.

Jeremiah's scream morphed into a dry heave. Pain radiated through his testicles and abdomen. He threw his head back and grinded his teeth.

"You ready to come out, demon!?" Millie grunted and huffed in sadistic joy. "Hurts, don't it! You wanna stay in my boy, huh? I'll keep at it!" She opened the Bible, then slammed it shut again.

Jeremiah tossed his head forward and vomited all over the Bible and Millie's hands.

Millie released the Bible and took a step back. "Good God Damn!" She shook her hands, flinging the bile now mixed with feces to the floor. "I seen this shit before." She nodded her head. "Definitely a goddamned demon. They puke like this when they getting ready to come out!" She spun in a circle with her hands raised, a lone stream of green diarrhea trickling down her forearm. "Praise you, Jesus, for your power! The hold of Satan is being broken!" She finished her worship, lowered her arms, and stepped back over to Jeremiah. "Come here, demon. We are just getting started."

Jeremiah took slow, heavy breaths. He spat on the floor and glared at Millie through his brow. "I ain't ... I ain't the one with the demon."

Millie's upper lip twitched, and she snarled. "Blasphemer!" She ripped the Bible from his lap and tossed it to the floor. She reached into the front pocket of her nightgown and retrieved some fishing line. Unraveling it, she dangled the string in front of his face.

"What ... what are you doing?" Jeremiah lifted his head, his body limp in the chair with exhaustion. The scent of shit and puke filled his nostrils.

Millie didn't answer. She reached back into her front pocket, and a kitchen knife appeared, the blade glimmering in the light. Millie cut the string, all the while humming "What a Friend We Have in Jesus." She held up the line and inspected it.

"That'll do." She smiled and leaned closer to Jeremiah. She stared him dead in the eyes. "I'm gonna set you free, son. I know you're in there somewhere. My precious baby boy." She caressed his cheek with the back of her hand and tilted her head. She batted her eyes, and the psychotic look disappeared. A compassionate gaze stared back at Jeremiah.

Jeremiah's stomach churned at her touch. The back of her hand was warm, and feeling her skin against his face made him want to vomit again. But all he managed was a whimper.

"Now," Millie said, removing her hand. "Spread them legs again. Let me get to the source of that demon."

Jeremiah's eyes widened in horror. "No. No, no, no, Momma!"

Millie bolted upright. "Demon! Don't you disobey me! I command you in the name of Jesus to spread them legs!"

Jeremiah shook his head in anger. "No! Leave me alone!"

"Yeah, there you are, demon. I got you, motherfucker!" Millie reached down and grabbed the Bible from the floor. She spread Jeremiah's thighs and stuck the book longways between them, keeping his legs open.

Jeremiah's panic and fear turned to anger. "I hate you! I fucking hate you! You crazy bitch!" He spat in her face.

Millie flinched as Jeremiah's liquid disdain splattered on her face. Her eyes bulged, and her fat cheeks glowed red. She wiped the spit off with her hand, then slapped the fire out of Jeremiah.

His ear burned, and all he heard was a loud ringing in his head. As he tried to clear the haze and let the bells in his eardrums settle, he felt Millie grab hold of his penis. The cobwebs faded, and he looked down at his crotch.

Millie worked in a mad frenzy, circling the fishing line around his tip. She tied it off and, with the slack in her hand, stepped back to admire her fisherman's knot.

Jeremiah's tip started to turn a dark purple. The line dug in deep, and the skin between the circular patterns of the string swelled. His penis ached and pulsated as the circulation was cut off.

He couldn't speak. The words wouldn't form. He stared down at his crotch in fright and screamed.

Millie gave the line a hard yank and held it taut. Jeremiah thought his pecker would rip from his crotch. He stared down at his manhood, whimpering. His penis had been stretched out like a glob of Silly Putty. The line squeezed his tip so tight it felt like it would tear loose or explode. "Momma, Momma, Momma! Stop, stop, stop! It hurts! Oh, God! Please!"

Millie set the knife down near the stove then tied the end

of the line around the refrigerator handle. She picked the knife back up and put it in her front pocket. She plucked the line like tuning a guitar string. "That'll hold."

She wobbled over to Jeremiah and removed the Bible from between his legs and continued the exorcism. She got down on her knees and stared at Jeremiah's outstretched penis. "You faggot demon, I command you to get out of my son's pecker! Now!"

Nothing happened.

Jeremiah pleaded with his mother. "Please, Momma! It hurts so bad!" He hung his head and wept. "You're hurting me, Momma." The tears flowed. "I just want Dad!" Jeremiah flung his head back and mourned. "Oh, God! I want my dad! Daddy! Daddy, please! Make her stop! Why did you leave me with her? Why?"

Millie gasped in horror and cut her eyes at Jeremiah. "How dare you! What? You calling for the dead now? Trying to speak to them? That's a sin too! Necromancy! Talking to the dead! God damn you, son! How many demons you got in you, huh? Where did they all come from?" She stared ahead, thinking. Millie gave her head a slow shake. "This is way worse than I thought. Way, way worse." She stood to her feet. "This is gonna require some more prayer."

Mille exited the kitchen and headed to her bedroom, leaving Jeremiah in the chair with his penis tied in the fishing line.

JEREMIAH PASSED out from shock and exhaustion thirty minutes later. He didn't know how long he slept. When he awoke, the sun's rays peeked through the blinds from the kitchen window above the sink. His body ached, and stiffness had set into his shoulders. He wiggled his wrist and his ankles, then winced. The rope burned the skin underneath, leaving it raw. He opened his dry, cracked lips and ran his tongue across them.

God, he was thirsty. A drop of water. Just one drop was all he wanted. And food. His stomach growled and rumbled. As he daydreamed about chugging a nice, cold glass of water, the pain in his crotch hit him full force.

"Oh, shit!" He had forgotten his mother tied his tip with fishing line. He closed his eyes. He didn't want to look. He feared how bad it would be. He knew if he glanced down, it would send him right back into shock. But he couldn't help it. He opened his eyes.

And screamed.

The tip of his penis had darkened to a charcoal-gray color.

"Ohmygod, ohmygod, ohmygod!" Panic sank its fangs deep into his soul, releasing its venom of dread.

Millie heard his screams and came stampeding into the kitchen. "Demon, you're still in my boy!" She finished off the powdered donut in her hand, leaving white remnants on the side of her lips. She smacked away as she talked. "You can't stay in him forever." She licked her fingers one by one, being sure to extract every last crumb of her snack.

"Momma, please let me go. It hurts so *bad*." Jeremiah shifted his eyes towards his penis.

"Damn right it hurts, demon." Millie crossed her arms. "You know what the apostle Paul says in Romans 6?"

Jeremiah's eyes widened, and he shook his head.

"Well," Millie said, uncrossing her arms. "Let me read it to you." She walked towards Jeremiah, circled behind him, and grabbed the large ivory Bible off the kitchen table. She must have placed it there after he passed out. She circled back around and stood before him. Millie opened the Bible.

"Romans six and thirteen. Neither yield ye your members as instruments of unrighteousness unto sin." Her voice escalated. "But yield yourselves unto God, as those that are alive from the dead." A sadistic madness twinkled behind her eyes as she continued. "And your members as instruments of right-eousness." She breathed so hard now it was like she slurped air. "Unto God!" She slammed the Bible shut with a thud. "Hear that, demon!" She waved her finger. "Unto God! Unto God! Unto God!"

Millie dropped the Bible onto the floor, and a hollow thud rang through the kitchen. "You are not using your little prick as an instrument of righteousness because it is demon-possessed!" Millie plucked the fishing line.

Jeremiah shrieked in agony.

"That penis belongs in a vaginal opening! Not in the ass of another man!" She plucked the string again. "And, demon, if you don't come out, I'm just gonna make sure you ain't got no instrument to play anymore." Millie left the Bible on the ground and walked out of the kitchen.

Jeremiah closed his eyes as tears cascaded down his face. There was fear and then there was unending, chaotic dread. The former did not compare to the latter. Hysteria. Yes. That was the state he was in. Anxiety collapsed down on him like an emotional avalanche. Trapped. Helpless. Left at the mercy of the unmerciful. His mother wouldn't stop until she killed him.

His emotional state shifted from an ebb and flow of spine-tingling trepidation to volcanic wrath. And in between, there was grief, sorrow, and despair. His broken heart, already fragile from the passing of his father, teetered on the edge of collapsing. His mental instability ran a close second. Depres-sion over losing the only person who ever showed him uncon-ditional love filled his mind like storm clouds, blocking out all rays of hope. Then there was the trauma of what he endured at the present. Mentally, he walked a tightrope … and he didn't know how much longer he could stay balanced.

All he wanted was his mother to love him and accept him.

Right now, what he wanted the most was to be out of the fucking chair and have his manhood back untethered.

Millie left Jeremiah tied to the chair for two more days. The wounds from the rope burns grew infected, and the tip of his penis turned black as ash. Dehydration set in, and the hunger pains made his stomach feel as if it cannibalized itself. He drifted in and out of consciousness, staying awake long enough to hear his mother read more Bible verses to try and cast the demon out.

The third night, Millie entered the kitchen and flipped on the light. Jeremiah stirred, and his eyelids fluttered. He gazed out as his mother with sunken, bloodshot eyes. She stood there eating a bag of pork rinds and staring at him with disgust.

"You ready to leave, demon?" She shoved a handful of pork rinds in her mouth and chomped away.

Jeremiah let out a faint moan.

She crumpled the bag closed, and the crinkling sound made Jeremiah twitch into full consciousness.

"Water ... please, Momma." He smacked his dry lips.

"Demons don't get thirsty. Now, I know you're a liar." Millie stuffed the bag of pork rinds into the pocket of her nightgown. She moseyed over to Jeremiah and leered down at him with her lip curled in disgust. "You stink like something awful, demon. That must be the hell sweating out of ya." She tilted her head to the side, the rolls in her neck expanding, and inspected his penis. "It's time. Wake up, demon."

Jeremiah blinked a few times. "I'm thirsty."

Millie cocked her arm back and let her hand fly. She slapped him right across the cheek. "I said wake the fuck up, demon!"

Jeremiah's body jerked, and he cried out in pain. He was wide awake. "Momma, please. I won't be gay no more, I promise."

"Oh, honey," she said and patted his head. "That's good. That's real good. But as long as the demon is in you, you don't stand a chance. We gotta get it out." She caressed his cheek. "I'm doing this for your own good. I love you." She kissed him on the forehead. "We just gotta do this one last thing and it will be gone for good, okay?"

Jeremiah gave rapid nods and sniffed. "Oh ... okay, Momma."

She turned her back to Jeremiah and walked towards the fridge. She paused at the handle and untied the fishing line. She made circling motions with her hand, wrapping the line around her fingers. She gripped it tight, then faced her son. "In the name of the Father, Son, and Holy Spirit! Come out of my boy!"

Millie yanked the line with all the power her 250-pound body could muster.

Jeremiah watched in horror as the blackened, dead tip of his penis ripped away from the rest of his cock. It ripped off with such force, it flew like a projectile towards his mother, slapped against the bottom of the refrigerator door, then bounced to the floor.

Jeremiah stared down at his half-castrated penis in disbelief. The end was dried over with a hardened scab. It resembled a flesh-colored sausage with the tip cut off. Fear, trepidation, panic, terror, hysteria—these were all just words. The emotions in Jeremiah were indescribable. His mind snapped like a brittle twig. Reality collapsed in on itself, and his mind dwelled in a static in-between.

He sat speechless, gawking at his deformity. His eyes bugged from their sockets, his mouth hung open, and his bottom lip trembled.

"Hot damn," Millie shouted. "We got it!" She twirled the line around her finger and lifted the blackened tip off the floor. It spun in a circle and dangled like a yo-yo. She raised it to eye level. "Look at that fucking demon head." Her smile stretched across her face in a crescent moon shape.

Jeremiah looked out at his mother. She held the demon head by the string and walked towards him. The tip of his penis rocked back and forth like a pendulum as she approached. "There it is, son!"

She swung it in front of his face as if she tried to hypnotize him. Jeremiah's eyes tracked the movement.

Then he saw it.

The demon was real. Glowing orange eyes stared back at him. Under the eyes, on a blackened strip of flesh between the layers of strings, were jagged white teeth. A pink serpent tongue flickered behind the teeth.

Jeremiah's face came to life. "We got it! We got it, Momma! I see it! I see it! It ain't dead yet. Kill it, Momma! Kill it!"

Millie jerked the severed penis tip away from Jeremiah. She threw it to the ground and raised her foot. She stomped it multiple times with her heel until it was flattened mush. "Did I get it? Is it dead now?"

Jeremiah leaned his head forward as far as it would go and peered down at it. He nodded. "Yeah, I think so."

"Oh, praise Jesus," Millie screamed, raising her hands. "Praise God!"

"I'm healed, Momma. Can you cut me loose?"

Millie dropped her arms and tilted her head. "Oh, baby. Of course we can." She slipped the knife from her front pocket and cut Jeremiah free.

His body relaxed, and he sighed in relief. Millie stood in front of him and set the knife on the floor. She got on her knees and embraced her son. "Oh, darling. You're free! You're free from that nasty demon!" She released him. "Now, let's get you cleaned up and get some food in you." She backed away to let Jeremiah rise to his feet.

Jeremiah stood on shaky legs. He gazed at his mother, smiling. Then his smile turned to an expression of fright. "Oh my God, Momma!"

Millie noticed her son's alarm and grabbed him by the shoulders. "What? What, honey?"

In Jeremiah's broken psyche, Millie's face turned demonic. Her eyes were gone. Large, black horns protruded from her eye sockets, curving around the top of her head. All the skin on her face had grown ashen in color. Her ears were pointy and elongated. The teeth in her mouth had changed also; they were glassy and opaque with jagged edges.

"The demon's in you!" Jeremiah remembered the knife. He dropped to one knee and scooped the knife from the floor. As he rose to his feet, he brought the knife in an upward motion.

The blade sank deep into Millie's throat, all the way to the handle. She let out gargle-coated screams. Her eyes swelled with fright, and she clasped her hands around her neck.

Jeremiah sawed away with the knife, cutting through flesh and tendons. The dark blood flowed as crimson water. It cascaded down Millie's chest and soaked his hands. He kept sawing until he reached the other side of her neck. He dislodged the blade and gazed at the parted flesh. It smiled back at him, and Jeremiah knew he had conquered the demon. He stepped back and let Millie's body collapse to the floor.

On the floor, next to Millie's bleeding body, he heard laughter.

"What? Who's that?" His eyes searched the floor. "You!"

His mother hadn't vanquished the demon in his penis. The face of the demon remained in the mashed, blackened tip, and it mocked him with laughter.

"Oh, it's funny, is it!" He grabbed the string and lifted the

24

demon off the floor. "I'll end you once and for all." Jeremiah walked over to the stove next to the kitchen sink, string in hand. He opened the cabinet, pulled out a frying pan, and turned on the burner. He placed the pan on the heat and waited for it to get hot. When the temperature was ready, he placed the demon in the pan.

The head sizzled, and the demon shrieked. The smell of burning, decaying flesh filled the kitchen. He rotated the demon, cooking it through on all sides. When the demon stopped screaming, Jeremiah lifted it by the string from the pan.

He tipped his head back, opened his mouth, and lowered the demon to its doom. He chomped away, chewing the rubbery flesh until it broke into several pieces. He removed the string from his mouth and swallowed.

"Ahh," he said and wiped his mouth. "No more demon."

"That's what you fucking think!"

The voice came from right underneath him.

"What the—" He looked down at his bare feet. "Oh my God!"

The big toe on his right foot wasn't a big toe anymore. It was a demon head. It looked the same as the one he saw in his mother.

"You can't get rid of me! I'm in you! I'm part of you forever," the face said.

"No! No, no, no!" Jeremiah ran out of the kitchen, past the table, and went into the garage. He swiped the garden shears hanging on the back wall.

The demon in his toe mocked him the entire time.

Jeremiah sprinted back into the kitchen. He plopped his naked ass down in a puddle of blood next to his mother. He stretched out his foot and positioned the blades of the shears around his big toe.

"Fuck you," the demon said.

"No," Jeremiah screamed. "Fuck you!"

He closed the handles with all his might. The blades met, and the sound of snapping bone echoed through the kitchen. The demon head tumbled to the floor, and blood spurted from his foot. Jeremiah yelped in agony.

He tossed the sheers to the side, then leaned up and grabbed the demon head from off the floor. It was still alive. Its tongue flickered, and its orange eyes glowed.

"God damn you," Jeremiah yelled. He shoved the demon head in his mouth and chewed. He worked and worked, gnawing the skin away from the nail and bone. He swallowed the skin first, followed by the nail and bone.

His foot throbbed, but he was relieved. Relieved the demon had been vanquished.

"No more." He shook his head. "Please, no more! I'm not gay! I'm not gay! The demon is gone!"

He pulled himself off the floor and grabbed a hand towel from the kitchen drawer. He sat back down on the floor and wrapped it around his wound, trying to stop the bleeding.

"It's never over, faggot!"

Another voice. This one was close. Too close. He glanced down at his stomach. "Holy fuck! Fuck, fuck, fuck!"

From his belly button down was a demon mouth. His mutilated penis had morphed into its tongue. Same as the toe. Same as his mother's face. His nipples were no more. The orange demon eyes stared up at him. Slits formed in his stomach, and they flapped as the demon breathed.

Jeremiah threw his head back and wailed. "Oh, God! God, help me! Why won't it stop! Daddy! Daddy, I need you! I hate myself! I'm so sorry I'm gay! I'm sorry, God! I'm sorry, Daddy! Please!"

Jeremiah scurried to his feet. He ran to the counter and opened another drawer next to the stove. He pulled out a pen and a piece of paper. He scribbled some things down, then put the pen back in the drawer and left the paper on the stove. He limped through the kitchen, grabbed the shears, and hobbled upstairs to his bathroom.

Jeremiah stood in front of the mirror. The demon face stared back at him.

"I'm part of you now," it said.

Jeremiah gnashed his teeth. "No! I'm not gay!" He opened the shears and positioned it around one of his nipples now turned demon eye. He slammed the handles, and the blade closed. The eye popped off and fell onto the bathroom counter. Jeremiah screeched in pain as the blood flowed down his chest.

"I'm not gay!" He picked up the demon eye and put it in his mouth. He chewed, then swallowed.

He repeated the action with the other eye.

Jeremiah gazed at himself in the mirror. The demon eyes were gone, and the sockets looked as if they cried blood.

"I'm still here, you queer!" The demon mouth on his stomach moved as it spoke. His mangled penis flopped and danced.

Jeremiah growled in anger. He placed the blades of the shears around the demon tongue. "I told you, fucker! I'm! Not! Gay!"

The blades met around the tongue, slicing through the skin like air. The demon tongue tumbled to the ground, and blood pumped from the wound. It flowed in waves, splattering all over the tile floor. Jeremiah grew faint, his knees buckled, and he crashed to the floor. He was weak, but he had enough in him to finish the job.

As he lay there, he wrapped his fingers around the demon tongue. He brought it to his mouth and proceeded to consume it like a skin-encased banana.

Blood covered his chest, his legs, and the floor. "I ... I'm not ... gay." He pulled himself up using the tub and leaned against the outside. "Almost ... free ... God ... I pray You accept me ... love me once I get it all out, will You?"

Jeremiah glanced down at his lower abdomen. The demon mouth was still there. Missing a tongue, but it still remained. The shears rested at his feet. He leaned forward, reached past his injured toe still wrapped with the hand towel, and grabbed them. He closed the handle, making the blades meet. He raised the shears into the air and let them hover over his stomach.

"I ... I'm not ... I'm not ... gay!"

He jabbed the blade into a spot below his belly button. He felt his consciousness leaving his body. He had to hold on. Just one more minute. He had to get rid of the demon. He worked the blade, making the hole larger,. He removed the sheers and tossed them behind him into the tub. He reached into the demon mouth and started to pull its insides out.

Jeremiah brought his intestines to his mouth. He held the tube in his hands and bit into it. He tore a piece off and chewed. The demon tasted like metal mixed with shit.

"Do you ..." He coughed and gagged, spewing up blood. "Do you love me now, God?"

Jeremiah's consciousness faded to black. His arms dropped to his side, and the intestines fell around his neck.

His bleeding, mutilated body lay on the floor, and his green eyes stared out into nothing. But he was free from the demon. His mother had made sure of it.

CASEY EATON DROVE down the highway to the Marshes' home. He served as the Youth Pastor for the First Baptist Church in town. It had been three days since the funeral, and he wanted to go check in and see how Jeremiah fared amidst all the sorrow.

Jeremiah Marsh.

The quiet, skinny kid who never said much at church. He avoided most social interaction except with him. Casey loved the kid. He held a special place in his heart. He didn't know why. There was something special he saw in Jeremiah. His dad was an amazing man. His mom, however? Casey thought she was mean, self-righteous, and would be one of the first persons God would throw into Hell on Judgement Day.

He turned his brown pickup down the Marshes' gravel driveway. He pulled up to the two-story farmhouse, killed the engine, and hopped out of the vehicle. He pulled his long, blond hair up into a ponytail and took out his piercings (the church didn't know he had them), then knocked on the door.

"Jeremiah! Mrs. Marsh! It's Casey." He placed his hands on his hips and waited for someone to answer. Seconds ticked by, and no one came to the door. He knocked again. "Hello? It's Casey from First Baptist." He looked, and Millie's old SUV was parked under the carport.

Casey waited another minute, then tried the handle. It was unlocked. He opened the front door and peeked in. "Mrs. Marsh? Jeremiah? It's Casey."

No answer. He heard the television blaring in the background, so he stepped inside. He looked to his left at the kitchen table, then glanced right.

All the breath left his body. "Oh, God! Jesus!"

Blood soaked the floor in the kitchen, and Mrs. Marsh lay in a crimson pool.

He ran over and knelt down beside her. He saw the gaping wound in her neck with the flesh and tendons exposed. He fell on his ass and scurried backwards, screaming. He scrambled to his feet and looked around, frantic. A paper near the stove caught his eye. He ran over and picked it up. His eyes searched the note as he read parts of it aloud.

"... my mom found out I was gay ... she tried to get rid of the demon ... she cut it out of me ... it entered her ... I cut it out ... it came back into me ... I had to go finish the job upstairs ..."

Casey dropped the letter. He sprinted out of the kitchen and upstairs. "Jeremiah! Jeremiah! Don't!" He rounded the corner and ran into Jeremiah's room. Dread over what he would find filled his heart.

Jeremiah wasn't in his room.

He saw the door to the bathroom cracked.

Time slowed to a crawl for Casey. He took slow, shaky steps towards the door. "Jeremiah," he whispered. Casey pushed the door open.

What his eyes saw evaporated all the strength out of his body. He caught himself on the counter and lowered his body to the floor.

"Oh, God! No! No, no, no, no, no!"

Jeremiah's dead body lay bleeding out all over the tile floor. His intestines had been pulled out and draped over his neck, and his nipples were sliced off. His penis was gone, and a rag had been wrapped around his big toe. Jeremiah's green eyes stared out into the void.

With tears streaming down his face, Casey crawled over to Jeremiah's corpse. He scooped him up in his arms and rested his head on his chest, weeping.

"Oh, God! What did she do to him? What did she do ...?" He ran a hand through Jeremiah's curly hair. "You were loved just as you are. God loved you! Oh, God, how He loved you!" He sniffed and wiped the tears from his face. "This has to stop!" He threw his head back and prayed. "Dear God! Please! Make the hate stop ... just make it stop already!" He hung his head again and wept, his tears mixing with Jeremiah's blood.

"Just make it stop. Just ... make ... it ... stop."

TED BUNDY

"I mean there's so much more to me than this guy that goes around doin' those crazy things... So much more"

— Ted Bundy

OUT ON A LIMB.

BY M ENNENBACH

"Chow is done, boys," Juarez said over the com.

"I don't think she has any idea what chow is. She has the magical ability to turn anything into boot leather," Dixon said with a sigh.

I just nodded with a grin.

And then everything went to shit.

Proximity alarms rang out.

"I thought you said this path was clear when you set it!" Dixon yelled.

I didn't respond. He knew as well as I did that the course was clear. Any abnormalities were autocorrected by the nav computer. The system took care of everything.

Except when it didn't.

"Dropping out of near light speed! Prepare for impact!" Dixon announced.

I stared at the screen and tried to make sense of what I saw. "It looks like an—"

Everything else was swallowed as, simultaneously, the hull was breached and the nanosuit formed around my body. Two equally horrifying extremes at once: the scream of steel being torn and then nothing at all.

". . . yon . . . ere?" Juarez said as the coms connected.

"I am?" I replied as I tried to get my bearings.

"And Dixon?" Juarez asked.

I watched Dixon's torso spin in zero gravity. His blood poured out in perfect spheres, the same as when the schooner slashed down the underbelly of the albino space whale to spill its guts into the embrace of nothingness.

"Dixon didn't make it," I said. "Neither did the bridge. Meet me at the auxiliary bridge so we can figure out how fucked we are."

"What did we hit?" Juarez asked.

I didn't want to say what I saw on radar. It was impossible.

"I don't know," I muttered.

"On the way to the aux. We can figure it out there," Juarez said.

I surveyed the wreckage through the flickering gold haze of the shielding. The side of the bridge where Dixon had sat was an empty hole into space. Arcs of electricity flared in white-blue against the darkness.

"You there?" Juarez called.

"On my way," I answered, trying to get my head focused.

I was on the verge of shock, my mind looping Dixon's detached torso in a slow pirouette where the remainder of the cockpit had once been, and felt my conditioning kick in. I didn't feel concussed, but adrenaline and the rush of stims from my suit pushed my body into action. Once I was through the blast door, there was no time to think about Dixon or impossibilities in space. They were carefully categorized and filed away until the only sound was the refresher kicking cool air into the junker.

When my heartbeat sounds so loudly in my ears, I long to tear the offending muscle free from the ivory cage.

I took a deep breath and entered the secondary bridge. It was a redundancy but a crucial one.

"We've got several hull breaches. Emergency beacon has been deployed," Juarez read off the display. She looked at me with wide eyes. "What in the fuck happened?"

I shook my head. "An asteroid field? I don't know for sure. I thought I saw something right before everything went to hell."

Juarez frowned. "Pirates? This is an empty expanse; there is nothing out here to see."

"An arm," I said softly.

"An arm? Awfully small to cause this kind of damage, don't you think?" Juarez rebutted with a laugh.

"I don't know what it was. Do we have any external cams still?" I asked.

Juarez tapped a few different monitors. "Three. Two rear facing, one forward." Juarez whistled. "You weren't lying about the asteroids. Fuck. They are all around us. How does an asteroid field just appear? There isn't a planet close enough to explain the debris."

I moved over and looked at the display. I tapped the screen. "Those aren't asteroids. Look at them."

"They appear liquid; perhaps mercury?" Juarez asked, confused.

"Sensors say high iron content," I answered. "This doesn't seem possible."

"It cannot be. If these reading are correct, those asteroids aren't asteroids at all. They are gigantic drops of blood," Juarez said. "Could it be from Dixon?"

I shook my head. "It was just his torso left. The human body doesn't have enough blood in it to make *one* of those. There are at least twenty out there."

"Where would that much blood come from? And why hasn't the ambient radiation destroyed it?" Juarez questioned.

"From a giant amputated arm," I said. "The most obvious answer, despite being illogical, may be correct."

"Okay. Suppose you're right. There is a giant disembodied arm floating in space. What did it come off of?" Juarez asked.

"Worse—is whatever, or whoever, still close?" I asked in reply.

Juarez opened and closed her mouth a couple times but remained quiet.

"We have propulsion still. Secondary is at sixty percent. We won't make it anywhere quickly, but we can limp on, hope someone catches our beacon," I suggested.

Juarez nodded. "I don't want to stay here any longer than we have to."

I looked at her. "We need to bring Dixon in."

"Do we? We know what is possible out here. There is a reason they require a beneficiary on each contract. Dixon wouldn't hesitate to get himself to safety after an event; we shouldn't either," Juarez stated calmly.

She was right. Probably. Sometimes, there is a disconnect between right and what is right. Perhaps I should've spoken up.

"The blood field is pretty dense," I said instead. Coward.

Hindsight is a bitch, isn't it, Dixon?

"It sure is, Donny."

"Donny!" Juarez yelled as she snapped her fingers.

I looked around, confused for a moment. I nodded. "Yeah. Let's do this."

I stared at the monitor and tried to find a route out of the undulating asteroid-sized globules of blood floating around us. This made zero sense. It should have been literally impossible. But trying to enforce logic on reality has proven time and time again to be a fool's pursuit. Centuries of interstellar travel had shown no signs of complex life forms anywhere but those which escaped the death rattles of Earth.

"Do you really think you saw an arm floating in space?" Juarez asked.

"Yeah, a fucking arm?" Dixon added.

I shook my head uncertainly. "I don't know."

I feathered the accelerator, and the ship shuddered. The roiling blobs of crimson began reacting in unison all around us.

"What the fuck?" Juarez asked as she stared at the screen.

I shrugged, not quite trusting myself to speak. Theoretically, we should be able to just fly through the liquid. But something, perhaps the floating torso of Dixon (which I knew was just outside ship), screamed to avoid contact. As we moved forward, the asteroids began to deform as they pulled in closer.

"The scanner is detecting quite a bit of motion in the core of the droplets," Juarez announced.

Droplets. I wanted to laugh. These things were the size of a small apartment back on Harrison 3, the backwater planet where I grew up. It was no longer there, just a field of space debris where a civilization had once flourished. Another casualty of mankind's second greatest ability: war.

Then the strangeness was compounded further as the asteroids convulsed and spikes began to jut out from them toward the ship.

"What in the fuck is happening!" I shouted, jerking the yoke to avoid an incoming spike.

Juarez didn't respond as klaxons wailed around us. I looked

up to see her staring at me in shock. The sharp tip of a blood dagger came from the ceiling of the ship, straight through her shoulder, and through the floor. Her mouth moved, but all that escaped was a death rattle, and her mask suddenly filled with red.

"Another corpse to abandon," Dixon whispered.

I was frozen in place. The reality of the situation was folded into the all-consuming horror as the blade shifted mercurially in front of me, sending small fingers of blood to run over my spacesuit. There was a sense of pressure on my chest and limbs, but I was paralyzed by fear as it coalesced around me.

I closed my eyes, unwilling to stare death in the eyes as I went.

The ship split all around me as I stood in the center of a magician's illusion where swords pierced everything. And when I finally opened my eyes once more, I was suspended in the liquid, floating in space.

Dixon's corpse slowly spun in front of me in lazy circles.

Would he spin for eternity out here? Was this the secret to the perpetual motion machine? A torso bombarded by radiation, slowly cooking until the end of time.

This was when I lost consciousness and fell into the maroon-tinged emptiness of space.

*

I woke with a start to the low oxygen alarm in my suit chiming, only to find myself inside of one of the giant globules, drifting through space. There was no sense of motion, but the steady change of angle from starlight to starlight told me it occurred. I forced myself to turn, and a sensation similar to what I imagined being in the womb must be like rippled over me. All around me, the rest of the asteroid belt of blood was drifting with us, called somewhere upon solar winds.

The heads-up display showed ten percent oxygen remained.

I had never given any real consideration to my inevitable end. Not since the aerial bombardment fell as our vessel left the atmosphere of Harrison 3. I felt adrenaline spike as cold sweat covered my body. My pulse quickened, and my only thought was this was going to burn through the minuscule stores of oxygen remaining. I tried to calm myself, going through the various training exercises they gave us before sending us into the vacuous asshole of space.

My guess is the instructors had never been ensconced in blood while floating toward an unknown hell, untethered from reality. Either that or they were just shit at their jobs. I didn't really know for certain.

Then I saw it floating in front of me. An arm the size of a planet. A tubular planet, admittedly, but shape didn't take a meter off the enormity of the detached limb.

What kind of wound draws the blood back to it? None I had ever experienced.

"Makes you think, doesn't it?" Dixon asked, but I ignored him.

"He doesn't understand. Not yet," Juarez added.

I ignored her as well. They weren't there. Not really. I knew this. What do they call those dreams where you know it is a dream yet you're swept along with the insanity?

Chances were just as likely that I had been impaled by a blood spike. Or the ship has been destroyed by actual asteroids. The final seconds of consciousness after the body has quit, where it is an eternity of swirling black.

This line of thought was enough to stop the worst of the palpitations; the shuddering force of my heart no longer shook my limbs.

Then the fifteenth oddest thing since waking occurred:

the alarm stopped beeping. The holographic display showed the oxygen levels slowly rise.

The analytical part of my mind—not the part screaming in abject terror but the calm slice of gray matter itself—whispered: If this was blood and still in liquid form, why would it not be saturated with oxygen? It was still bright red. I only knew as much about physiology as the AI had taught in school that I didn't sleep through.

I liked history mostly. Or when it was story time and the lights dimmed as images danced through the room.

The ships came loaded with all the essentials required: a full medbay with cutting edge AI doctors, atomic scramblers capable of making anything we may need while out for another long sojourn among the stars.

I always liked that word. Sojourn. It seemed hefty, as if it carried more weight than simply calling it interstellar flight.

"Fancy word for a fuckup," Juarez snarled.

I nodded. It was. I always liked words. I didn't always understand people as well, hence the decision to pilot junkers from port to port rather than pursue a position planet-side somewhere. I barely liked the excursions to space stations, preferring to remain aboard during refuel and repairs.

Floating alone in a sphere of blood in the irradiated nothingness made me reconsider crowds slightly.

"Level three autism makes for a helluva pilot but absolute shit as a conversationalist," Dixon and Juarez said in unison, just as they always had when my weird was coming on a little too strong.

I tried to block them out as the limb grew larger in my approach. The flesh, if it were flesh, had a ruddy brown color which was covered in dark, coarse hair. The part I find so difficult to convey—as solar winds made the hairs ripple, swaying like the tangerine canopy of the jungle planet, Miller

83C, as the lunar monsoons raged—is it only appeared as an arm due to perspective.

You're not even there, not really. Maybe one day, if my corpse is discovered and the last moments of madness are captured.

What will you think as you go through this impossibility?

Doesn't matter.

The suit recycled my sweat and waste. The blood provided oxygen.

"You should nap," Dixon murmured sleepily.

An acceptance washed over me. I would die soon. Either trapped in crimson or out on an impossible limb floating in space. I didn't dwell on the things I would never experience. Love. A floor that didn't vibrate along with the quasar engines.

"Those things were never in the cards for you. For any of us. We knew it when we became junkers," Juarez whispered.

She was right.

I decided sleep would conserve depleting stores. Nestled in a wobbling bubble of blood, I watched the beauty of the universe unfold around me and eventually slept.

*

I dreamt of a kitten. Orange and white with a pink nose. A little thing. I had never seen a cat before, not in real life. Cats and dogs were status symbols, and I was born to be a junker. But this dream kitten was mine. It curled in a ball on my chest and vibrated the same as the quasar engines, which was comforting. I was on a hammock, suspended over the Bullock Gorge as the triple suns set. The air was pure, no ozone discharge or body odor from being cramped at all times. Just the kitten and me.

The kitten opened one eye and looked at me. "The mortal mind was not made to comprehend the vileness of detached divinity."

I nodded. The kitten slept.

*

"Wake up, Donny," Dixon said.

I opened my eyes to see I had arrived. No longer did the monstrosity resemble an arm that ended in a hand large enough to hold a planet. Instead, I had woken at the edge of the jagged wound on an immense shard of bone jutting from the flesh. I felt my gorge rise as I peered over the edge to witness ragged flesh extending downward father than I could see, which looked like a ten-thousand-times-blown-up version of an art exhibit I snuck into as a child on Harrison 3—the artist vat-grew living slabs of meat in various shapes and designs. There were veins large enough to pilot ships into dribbling perfect spheres of blood, which deformed and floated en masse.

And then nothing but vertigo-inducing emptiness.

I carefully got down from the ivory perch to the ground I was too aware was actually flesh. There was a slight give to it, a spongey feel rather than the tautness I imagined it once held.

I didn't care for this line of thought.

"Feels fucking crazy," Juarez whispered with a giggle.

Hard to disagree with sound logic like that.

I'm not crazy. They aren't actually there. I have suffered severe mental and possibly physical trauma; this is just a coping mechanism and shock.

Am I actually on a floating arm in space?

This was where it got tricky.

"This sure as shit is happening, Donny. Don't try and work your way through this like a Pfeifferian Flatsnake. The question should remain: what could have possibly lost such an enormous limb?" Dixon calmly asked.

God.

Humans have proven to be the only truly intelligent creatures in the entirety of the known universe. There have been other life forms discovered, but none which exceeded the intelligence of, say, a Hussel Boar or the sentient stones of the Nickey Belt.

The ancient texts spoke of a creator which molded humanity in its image. Besides a few offshoot clusters in far-off sectors, these texts were discarded after Earth Prime was discovered far across the cosmos. Earth, the origin of the great Exodus, had been reduced to smoldering ruins and abandoned. It wasn't until it had become more myth than reality, we landed upon the precursor. This should have been cause for celebration, yet all it did was spark intergalactic war.

But God was discarded along with other myths once the true origin planet had been discovered.

"Maybe the creation myth never occurred on Earth at all. Perhaps it was a tale from across the universe. God is an astronaut, and somehow, after millennia, we found proof," Dixon whispered.

"Discarded divinity," I whispered back.

I realized at that exact moment, I envied Dixon and Juarez and their fast deaths.

"Trade you," Juarez snarled.

"What do you do now?" Dixon asked.

The hand. The arm was severed near the shoulder joint. I never actually saw the hand, just the outline. Perhaps it held some clues as to what had occurred. To what led me here.

The arm had its own weak atmosphere. Not enough to survive on but enough, here at least, to allow my suit to do the rest. My stomach rumbled loudly, thunderous in the silence of the sepulcher setting.

"Bet you wish you'd have eaten my chow now," Juarez said smugly.

I ignored her and stared down the vast expanse of bicep in front of me. I began moving down the shattered shoulder, where retracted muscle coiled, forming hills, the striations in makeshift paths in dusky skin. As I walked, the knowledge this planet was an arm became a schismatic juxtaposition compounded by adrenaline and hunger.

"You should yell to see if anyone is out there," Juarez suggested.

There wasn't, so I didn't.

"You have your blade," Dixon reminded me.

I didn't think he meant as a means of self-defense, but still, I let my palm rest upon the hilt momentarily. I wasn't nearly to the point of opening a vein yet.

Yet.

It was only a matter of time.

My stomach rumbled again.

"Technically, you ARE standing on meat. Not sure what kind of meat, but any port in a solar storm," Juarez offered.

I continued walking down the musculature, ignoring the intrusive thoughts of marbling. My heads-up display let me know I had plenty of oxygen. Water was going to be an issue, but that was a later concern. I magnified my view, yet only the vast expanse of biceps greeted me.

"I bet he doesn't see the elbow before going totally fucking crazy," Juarez helpfully said.

"He will be dead long before then," Dixon amended.

I put my head down and began walking.

*

Weeks later

"He made it to the elbow," Juarez said.

Her tone made me feel prickly, but I ignored the sensation. She wasn't there. Instead, I grabbed a handful of my beard and sawed it off with my knife. I hadn't succumbed to eating the flesh of this new world.

I tried. In my desperation, I sliced a chunk off and stood staring as the wound bled.

Somehow, against all logic, the detached arm was still somehow living.

It wasn't until I stood at the edge of a large pore—in all honesty, considering falling into it and ending my misery—when I saw something.

A skin mite. But on scale with the skin.

"Still think they taste like skiprat?" Dixon asked.

I shrugged as I tapped the hilt of my blade against the metal of my boot tip. I bit my lip in concentration as I waited for the spark to catch, the beard hair smoldering. I had grown proficient over time, learning which secretions hardened. The coarse hairs which sprang out randomly along the long bicep made for a decent fuel source, even if it smelled horrendous. Sweat accumulated around the great trunks of the hairs, allowing a source of water to be filtered by my suit.

As the skin mite sizzled in the burning hair, I realized it wasn't great, but it was manageable.

"He is staring off again," Juarez said.

I ate my mite silently.

The arm rotated slowly, enforcing a day-night schedule over the arid wasteland that was the upper arm. It took days before I found the first oasis at the base of a hair. The presence of sweat should have been upsetting on a limb forcibly removed, floating in the vacuum of space. I discovered my needle of acceptable impossibilities spun about on the dial, leaving me no way to frame the madness as anything except the new normal of existence.

"It's called shock. You're in survival mode still. The sheer absurdity of—" Juarez began.

"ENOUGH!" I shouted. Sort of. It was more a billowing croak after so long silent. Phlegmy. The word felt as if it tore from my throat.

The return to silence was unsettling. Oppressive. By the time I had realized how silent it was, the initial panic had faded, and yes, I probably slipped into a bit of a dissociative fugue in the hopelessness.

Now I tried to find a reason in the survivability of the situation. I could continue on. I would continue on. But why?

Why?

The least healthy thought was grasping for a reason to live beyond the fact I could.

Because I couldn't.

Fuck. I put out the flame and stared as the last embers winked out. I lay staring into the vastness of space, the billions of stars winking at me in ferocious delight.

I worried I ran Juarez off. Knowing full well she was never really there did not abate the anxiety. Anxiety was real.

Was that a reason to live?

I don't know how, but I managed to sleep.

*

I was sitting on the couch with a piece of string. I wriggled it across the floor like a Benetti eel.

The kitten crouched low to the floor, tummy rubbing the plastisteel as its little butt wiggled in the air. An orange and white flash and the kitten and string were in a ferocious struggle to the death on the floor.

A wet slapping against window frightened us both, and I stared in horror as a tentacled beast with row upon row of razored teeth slammed against the side of my home.

The kitten sat staring at me, the string and incomprehensible horror forgotten, and began licking its paw. It ran the paw across its face. "Did you think there would be no repercussions for ingesting divinity? Better to have starved slow. Better to have leapt off the wound."

I knew it was right.

"What is that?" I asked, pointing at the rampaging beast.

"The aftereffects of curiosity," the cat replied.

"Whose curiosity?" I asked, knowing the answer.

45

I wiggled the string again, and the cat pounced on my hand, a flurry of furious teeth and claws.

*

I woke to my hand bleeding. Rows of four slices, and small pinpricks of red welled up. I searched the area and found nothing.

"What the fuck happened to your hand?" Dixon asked.

I didn't know how to answer that. A dream cat?

Why didn't the figment of my imagination know?

"What makes marks like that?" Juarez asked in the pregnant silence. A touch of hurt in her voice rang under the curiosity.

I felt a migraine coming on behind my left eye. Soft but building in intensity.

I sat at the bend of the great arm. The elbow. There were long stretches where I lost sight I was not just lost on an alien planet. Moments like these brought the realization back down upon me with crushing force.

Was this God's arm? Had something managed to sever an appendage from the creator of everything?

I grew up a firm believer in nothing.

Now I stood at the great bend in an enormous limb of which I could not fathom the source. When all common-sense answers fail, there is only impossibilities left to ponder.

I tried not to think at all.

The only true escape from life is death.

Or so I had believed.

Ahead of me lay the great forest of gigantic hairs. I was still days, if not weeks from the forearm. I couldn't guess how long until the hand itself. I had shut off the distress beacon weeks ago. The same time I shut down the time and date stamp on my HUD. It was all meaningless. Nothing mattered except reaching the hand, where I was sure nothing waited for me.

"Think he finally lost it?" Dixon whispered.

"I hope so," Juarez snickered.

I had no way of knowing if I had or not. So it didn't matter. If you're completely mad and alone, you're still the sanest person in the world.

Or on a limb.

I laughed softly to myself as I forced my legs to move. The hand awaited.

*

Months later

Weeks after entering this new ecosystem, one where the coarse hairs trap in the sweat, forming a miasma of mist each morning, I found myself quite lost. The canopy above, swaying skyscraper-sized strands, blocked my once clear view of infinity.

"Each day begins with him moving in a different direction, while the hand grows no closer," Dixon remarked as I sat staring as if hoping to will the correct direction into view.

Juarez had been silent for a while now. She had begun whispering about the shadows incessantly throughout the day, until one day, she just stopped speaking. Dixon hadn't seemed to notice. Or maybe he still spoke to her and it was I who had been cut out of the loop.

I didn't care.

The follicle basins were teeming with mites, and the pathways between marshy sinkholes became a confusing labyrinth, a shadowy world where micro and macro are interchangeable terms for madness.

When I was a kid, there was a holo series they used to play about an adventurer named Eric who would get marooned on different unexplored planets. He would somehow manage to survive, and his escape beacon would call in a rescue ship in the nick of time each episode.

I considered turning the beacon back on, momentarily;

maybe somewhere out there, someone would detect the signal.

Rescue was a dream for the person I used to be.

Instead, I lowered myself into one of the oily ponds in the follicle basin and let the warmth wash over me. There was something in the pool, one of the oils, possibly, or another secretion suspended that remained invisible to my eye. The suit could tell me, but I had long since grown distrustful of the tools of man. This was no place for technology in anything but its most base form.

The secretion. It had a sensation similar to the fungi they traded in the more end-of-nowhere stops. But more visually stimulating.

It was no coincidence I began to lose my way not long after discovering this. And who could blame me? I was alone. Far enough from anyone or anything to continue the false clinging to hope for. I had the hand. This quagmire of a forearm.

And the heady visions were nice. It reminded me of watching those holos with my sister. I had so wanted to grow up to be Eric the Adventurer.

Fuck Eric. All he did was feed kids lies to turn them into junkers.

"Another bath? At this rate, we will never get to the hand," Dixon lamented as I settled in.

*

"If this works, we will be able to see exactly what the Big Bang was like," the scientist in a full white lab coat said excitedly to me.

I nodded. "And what if the force of impact is too great? We don't know exactly what the forces we are dealing with are capable of."

She laughed and patted my shoulder. "We have it all under

control, worry wart. This is a contained loop, buried underground."

I wasn't convinced. The idea of slamming two atoms into one another seemed like a bad idea. The big bang was theoretical at best, an explosion which laid the groundwork for the entirety of the ever-expanding universe. There was no way to tell if, even in a closed environment, this could be catastrophic.

I also didn't know how any of this information was mine. I didn't know a thing about atoms. Or slamming them together.

"Old Man Higgs would be freaking out right now," I said instead.

"This will revolutionize science!" she said as she reached in her pocket and pulled out a pen and made some notes on her clipboard.

The yellow lights that flashed around us took on a somber red shade.

"Particles launched," a somber voice intoned over the speakers.

Everyone in the room went silent.

I closed my eyes and braced for the impact I couldn't even see. There was a flash of light, and blinding pain shot through my left side. When I opened my eyes, I was floating in space. The source of the agony floated next to me. My arm, severed at the shoulder.

*

I splashed in the pool as I came back, clutching my now attached left arm. I could still feel the last remnant of sizzling pain flare across confused nerves.

I hadn't questioned the visions as real before. Nonsensical non sequiturs. Or so they seemed. I thought I was just high and escaping this hell momentarily.

What if it were real?

49

"You okay?" Dixon asked.

Was he actually there?

"Does Higgs mean anything to you?" I asked, my voice rasping like a file over my vocal cords.

"Higgs Boson? The God particle. We studied it briefly, but I didn't pay much attention beyond that. Why?" Dixon replied.

I didn't answer. I felt my acceptance begin to crumble.

Was I being called to the hand?

It seemed fully embracing insanity and fighting against it were two sides of the same cred.

I felt a renewed sense of purpose. Either there were answers at the palm or I was going to come back here and float until my body ceased to function, lost in impossible dreams. It didn't matter which, not really, it just felt good to be motivated.

"I don't know why he asked about it. Perhaps he has finally fucking lost it," Dixon said.

No one answered him. I considered it, but his ability to provide an answer I knew I didn't know made me feel as if I was more far gone than I needed to be to make the journey.

*

I found myself lost between the worlds as I struggled to find my way across the great forearm. My body seemed saturated by whatever it was floating in the follicle pools, and I began slipping in and out, unsure which was reality. I felt as if I were slipping linearly through time steadily backwards. From the moment of the severing, I slip-slided through different moments.

I was an old man theorizing atomic structure. Then a woman working in a factory sewing garments. A farmer. A soldier. A peasant. A duchess. My body trudged along as my mind was coursing through history, and I was only ever half aware in either realm. Which one of these lingering mental phantasms was reality? Was I a rough approximation of thousands of dissimilar souls, or one very lost junker roaming the detached arm of what was more and more likely to be not just a god but THE God, whom humanity had long since forgotten?

In my travels through other people's lives, I watched the focus of curiosity go from understanding the smallest forms of matter, to barely mattering, to pure survival, which was a dire reflection of my devolution from man to microscopic organism.

I began unravelling, untwisting the double helix of my own irradiated DNA, barely cognizant of the sweat forest of undulating hair in solar winds. Had I ever been anywhere else? Memories—a haphazard display of which I was only certain of living through a scant few—bombarded me.

"One foot in front of the other, the automaton treks toward destiny," Dixon murmured just outside the miasma polluting my mind.

I began to suspect Juarez had always been a figment. It had been months since she last spoke. Weeks. I didn't know. Time was a construct used to give a semblance of order to chaos, to trap life into easy-to-digest increments so we weren't driven mad by the full-throttle race toward death.

I wasn't even there.

I was crouched low to the ground in tall grass, a crude spear clutched in my sweating hands. There was something in the grass with me; I could feel it watching, preparing to attack.

I was a child being boarded onto one of two gleaming rockets as mushroom clouds raised in the distance over great domed cities on a world close to death.

In rare moments of lucidity, I pondered the flood of memories and knew instinctively they were all encoded into my very being. The memories of every single ancestor down my family tree were folded neatly into protein strands.

Man was not meant to harbor so many experiences. The cat was right. Defiled divinity pulsated all around me, through me, a cancer spreading which slowly erased who I was by forcing me to see everyone my contaminated blood had ever flowed within.

I don't know when I accepted all of this, if I ever truly did. The wonder of the visions had become another facet of hell of which I was forced to endure.

"One foot in front of the other," Dixon half sang mockingly.

I didn't realize my eyes were closed, and when I opened them, I saw Dixon standing near the base of a hair. He was indistinct, transparent. Briefly, I saw thousands of others staring at me. I closed my eyes again, tightly, and counted slowly to one hundred. When I opened my eyes again, they were all gone.

"How far have you traveled?" Dixon asked.

Mostly all gone.

*

I followed the curve of the wrist, having finally exited the forest of arm hair at the base of the wrist bone jutting into space. There was an incomprehensible level of frustration seeing the vast expanse of the back of the hand. I wanted to reach the palm and at long last fulfill this purpose which had so electrified me, only to realize the closer I came, the farther I was from any type of answer.

Once I skirted the edge of the bone mountain, the edge of the wrist gave me a view of infinity. Vertiginous in empty beauty, I wondered if I would simply fall into forever as I took my first hesitant step. Disappointingly, I continued walking, an inconsequential speck of stardust bathed in the blinding glory of his ancestors.

"I hoped he would drift into space," Dixon muttered.

He had grown angry as we left the forearm proper. I didn't know what had changed to cause this new demeanor. I don't think I cared either. I wasn't sure if I was here most of the time. Even now, the ruddy flesh around me was overlaid with an ancient civilization, and I marveled at the statues carved from pure white stone.

I wasn't anywhere, and somehow everywhere at the same time.

I was thankful for the delicacy of the wrist. Not from a structural standpoint as much as from it made the journey quicker.

"Hurry to your death, fucking idiot," Dixon whispered, his disembodied voice drifting among the statues.

I heard a chorus of laughter like leaves on a tree.

*

As I stood before the mountainous pads of the palm, all I felt was a bone-deep weariness. I wanted to lay down in the crease of the line that led like a valley into the gigantic hand itself. The absurdity of this mission, one bathed in madness and coupled in impossibilities, brewed an urge to laugh deep inside of me. I refrained, knowing once I began, I would likely never stop.

"He is smiling again for no reason," Dixon said softly.

As much as I hated having a figment drifting along beside me, I could not imagine the loneliness without him. I even missed Juarez and her shitty cooking.

I wondered if the answer I sought would provide me an escape. Or at least closure. I didn't know which sounded better. I could return to one of the backwater planets and write of this grand delusion. Find a woman and raise a child. Perhaps start a cult worshipping the great detached limb of God himself.

Or find out why I've lived a thousand frozen moments in other people's lives as I trudged on across the flesh expanse of an abhorrent chunk of flesh.

I didn't think I could ever really return to normality. I had never been there in the first place. A life of outrunning calamities man caused across the desolate universe. Long stretches of silence except the murmur of engines.

I couldn't give in to the exhaustion. Not now. Not so close to my imaginary goal.

Maybe I never left one of those follicle pools. Slowly being eaten by skin mites the size of howl bears from the Stockton nebula.

Or in a coma on the ship. Maybe I fell and hit my head. I was clumsy. Careless.

"Am I on life support?" I gasped, the act of speaking unfamiliar and painful.

"Is he talking to me?" Dixon asked.

"Yes. Is this real?" I replied.

"I think he is talking to me. That's even worse than the smile," Dixon sputtered in fright.

I sighed and pushed myself forward. One leg at a time. A step, then two. I followed the fleshy crease into the palm of God.

"The life line," Dixon said. *"Does he see the irony in it? Following the life line to his impending doom?"*

I did. I embraced it.

*

An eternity later

I used the tips of the gargantuan fingers to direct myself toward the center of the palm. There were no hairs to plumb for water or sustenance. The landscape of the palm was like a desert, minus the whipping silicate. Perhaps more like a glacier without the cold. It was vast and barren. I made small slits in the skin, letting the suit suck water and whatever nutrients it could from the seeping blood. It was no longer the vivid crimson which took down the ship or which sprayed from Dixon as his torso spun slowly in the vacuum.

I feared it was finally beginning to decompose. There were no signs of rot, yet the blood was more rust than vermillion.

This wasn't a concern for now.

The four fingers, half curled up to the heavens, were my focus. I don't know how long I roamed the flat land, marked by creases where the mighty hand had once articulated. But using the sensors of my suit, I triangulated a rough approximation of center and eventually found what I assumed to be the center of the great open hand.

You could set moons on each fingertip. Five moons glaring impassively at an exhausted fool. I longed to have someone to share the view with. But I had no one except Dixon, and he hadn't spoken much since I questioned him outside the open fist.

If this were truly the hand of the creator, I sat in the true birthplace of the universe itself. Did those fingers once grasp the essence of existence and force it to be?

The whorls of fingerprints in which entire civilizations could live and die gleamed in front of me.

"Hello? God? It's me, Donny. Donny Kilpatrick from Harrison 3? I'm here. I don't know why or how, but I made it. Please give me a sign I am where I am supposed to be," I asked the emptiness.

I sat, I don't know how long, waiting for an answer. None came.

"Was this all a fucking joke? An accident? Coincidence? Why am I here? Why did I live all those different lives? Please, God, I just need to know it wasn't all pointless."

At first, nothing happened. I sat there feeling like a fucking moron begging dead digits to give my life a purpose. I should have given up forever ago. There was no reason to have kept going. I had a good enough life in the forearm. Enough, at least, to while away. Plenty of food. Water. Shade.

What did I have here? The dispassionate fingertips and thumb of some mutated hand.

Then something happened. The pinkie finger twitched slightly.

"God?" I asked fearfully.

The only answer was a slight spasm of the thumb.

One by one, the fingers flexed slightly. I sat enthralled at the spectacle. I could feel the bones shift beneath me and the tendons stretch.

There was no sense of passage of time as the fingers seemed to slowly awaken. The palm distorted around me with the movement, the flat plains rippled, yet where I had chosen to sit remained an ocean of calm in the nascent chaos.

One by one, each finger stretched out, and I sat in the massive canyon, unable to see past the raised callused palm. This was it; whatever drew me here was culminating in this very moment. I could feel it. I felt giddy. I was probably the first person in untold millennia to witness the glory of God, even if the true majesty was limited to an arm ripped off and left to float in the middle of nowhere.

I was chosen.

The momentous occasion gave me hope. When, not if, I returned home, I would travel the universe and spread the gospel of this benevolent deity. I would teach of our Lord, my personal savior.

"I am ready, God. I see my purpose now. Thank you," I yelled hoarsely into the nothingness.

I felt the hand shifting again and smiled. I was heard. I was chosen.

The fingers bent upwards, the true immensity of each digit on full display, and I got to my knees and pressed my head down against the flesh and murmured my thanks.

But the fingers didn't stop moving. A great shadow fell

over me, and I stared up in anticipation. Would God speak to me? Explain all which occurred before?

Glee turned to horror as I realized the fingers weren't going to stop. I held out my hand and mimicked the motion of the giant hand.

I felt the snort of derision escape my throat as my hand made a fist. I watched the fingers descend, and I knew I had no hope of escaping the force strong enough to crush a planet like a piece of trash.

"See you soon," Dixon half chuckled.

HH Holmes

"I was born with the devil in me. I could not help the fact that I was a murderer, no more than the poet can help the inspiration to sing. I was born with the evil one standing as my sponsor beside the bed where I was ushered into the world, and he has been with me since."

—HH Holmes

SEE ME NOW

BY GAGE GREENWOOD

SEE ME.

Two years after a man walked into The Switch and Grille and shot my father, along with fifteen other patrons and staff members, I'm sitting on a stone ledge overlooking the Pawcatuck River, staring blankly at my reflection as it fractures within the wind-disturbed water. Across the Pawcatuck, Tanner's Mill, an old textile dyeing plant, sits boarded and hollow. It stares at me knowingly.

See me now, you motherfucker.

Behind me, a man walks by with two children flanking him. The kids are begging for ice cream, and the poor guy is doing his best not to crack. Not me, though. I am well-broken. No need to fight it. I could also go for some ice cream.

I see it more and more now, torn faces, tired eyes, and sagging smiles. I promise not to get political here, but this is all to be expected after 40 years of allowing eight companies to own everything. We can only be bought so often before we appear used. We are all well-thumbed books, but not by passionate readers. Our spines were cracked by those who wish to turn our pages to pulp, repurposed and spat out again.

None of that matters, I suppose. I'm just expressing that while I hate the man who shot my father, I don't fully blame him. He was a product. And he produced. Just as we all do in the end. A bomb, after all, is designed to explode. I abhor every fiber of him for it, but my hatred extends beyond him to the machinations of his creation, the pulleys and levers and conveyors, and the men who packaged him, and, most importantly, the ones who ran the shop as they do all shops, hiding behind their gates and forcing the rest of us to pull the levers that build the bombs that explode in our faces.

Yes. Ice cream sounds good.

I hop off the ledge and follow the two boys with their father, who has now relented and promised them soft serve cones. When we arrive at Willow's Ice Cream, a bell dings above the door, and the sad teenage girl behind the counter looks up from her phone to greet us with a smile. She probably suspects we're all together. For a teenager working a shit, thankless job for little pay, she's incredibly peppy, joking with the children and dutifully making their orders. I stand back with my hands in my pockets, watching it all unfold. I envy her. I forgot what it feels like to have kindness left inside me. Real kindness. Not the fake stuff. It's so obvious she enjoys making these kids happy.

After Beth serves the children their cones, the father sits with them at a nearby table, while I rock back and forth on my heels, hands still in my pockets, staring stupidly at the menu. I want ice cream. I do not know what I want. These two things can both be true.

I feel the sleek outline of my cellphone in my pocket. Maybe I should go.

The girl behind the counter, Beth, so claims her nametag, waits patiently for me, offering the same smile she gave the children. How does she do it? How does she manage a genuine facial expression? Sure, she's young, but she doesn't appear naïve. She has to know the world isn't going to get better.

As I debate between caramel swirl or cookie dough—none of that soft serve shit for me—people scream outside the shop. I turn in a flash because you never get used to the screaming, no matter how many times a day you hear it. The father whips out of his chair, creating a loud screech as the legs slide across the tiled floor. He scoops his children out of their seats and hides them behind him, but he does not move away. Instead, he stares out the window with me at the scene unfolding. Both of us have grown so accustomed to it all.

A man paces in front of the store across the street. Mackey's Hacky Sacks and Outdoor Games. The man is completely engulfed in flames. Like the folks who have now run across the road, he's screaming. Poor fool hadn't quite considered how much pain comes from lighting oneself on fire. And then, just as he falls to his knees, ready to give up the ghost, he shouts, "They already had my soul. Might as well have the body too." It's a strangely stubborn response from a person who wore regret on his flaming body just seconds before.

Once he's fully lying on the ground, tendrils of grey drifting off his crisped body, someone runs out of Mackey's with a fire extinguisher. Within seconds, the body disappears behind a sea of white foam.

It takes a few moments for the smell to hit us. The father cringes as it wafts in, and one of the little boys tosses his cone in the garbage, no longer hungry. The smaller child keeps licking, though, trooper that he is. When it comes into my nostrils, I hold back a gag, despite being prepared for it. I've smelled it dozens of times now, and it never gets easier.

It's such a hard thing to describe, burnt flesh. Painfully powerful, putrid, and thick. I never knew that man, but I can taste him.

Sometimes our nose has a stronger memory than we do, and I know the scent won't be leaving me anytime soon. I turn back to the girl, who's staring out the window with horror in her eyes. Her face tells me she hasn't had the luxury of seeing this before. Soon, she'll see it enough times, it'll all blend together, and she won't even remember where she was when she first witnessed it.

"I changed my mind," I say.

She nods, not looking at me, still staring at the scene across the street. The shop man who had used the extinguisher douses the dead body in water to remove the foam blanket. Pieces of the scorched body unearth.

Beth's smile disappeared. I doubt it'll ever come back.

I sigh and head for the door, but before my hand can grip the handle, the sirens come. Loud, piercing alarms ring from everywhere, down the road, up the road, in the shop. The people outside go back to screaming as they scramble for shelter. The father pins his children to the wall, wild-eyed, completely lost on what to do.

"What's happening? It's way too early for those."

He's right. It doesn't make sense, but I'm not interested in figuring it out. Besides, I have my suspicions, and I don't want to come to terms with them yet. For now, we need shelter, and we need it fucking quick. A shop with a glass front façade won't cut it. I turn to Beth. Luckily, the alarms shook her from her daze. "Is there a basement? A back door? Anything?"

She nods, at first just a slight one, but as she recognizes the severity of what's happening, she shakes violently. "Yes. A basement."

"Well, let's go," I say, waving to the father to let him get in front of me. He's got kids, after all. Maybe I do have some humanity left in me.

Beth, the father, the kids, all of them dart their eyes everywhere, clearly slowed down by confusion in the chaos. In the distance, people shriek, and the sound of it, the hyper-intensity and desperation, tells me they aren't screaming in fear but pain. The beasts are clawing them apart.

Beth opens a door behind the counter, leading down a thin flight of stairs. It's too dark to see how far they go, but it's a steep descent. I'm last in line as we single-file down the steps. Musty basement smell fills my nose, which I'm thankful for after the burnt human aroma. The closer to the bottom we get, the more my eyes adjust to the dark. It's a small room filled with boxes. They're piled in stacks, many of them soggy at the bottom, causing the piles to slant. Because of these, the room is made even smaller, more mazelike. If the beast comes, we'll have plenty of spaces to hide, but our covers would be fragile and way too easy to give ourselves away with a gentle bump to one of the boxes. The entire contents of the room could topple like dominos.

As Beth clicks on a small overhead bulb, I notice the children's faces for the first time since the man lit himself on fire. Their cheeks are tear stained, and new beads form in their eyes. The dad must have trained them well because they haven't made a peep, not even a sniffle. I hear my own father's words in my head: "When the bells ring, shut the fuck up."

One of the kids says, "Shouldn't we turn the light off?"

Beth whispers, "I'll click it off if we hear them come in."

Luckily, the beasts aren't subtle. They won't turn the doorknob and sneak in; they'll crash through the windows, snarling and barking. In other words, we'll have advanced notice if they get close.

I extend my hand to the father. "I'm Jason."

He nods. "Bradley." He points to the taller boy. "This is Brayson." And then to the younger. "And this is Finn."

It felt silly to make introductions at such a stressful time, but if I needed to shout out instructions on the fly, I didn't want to waste precious time using descriptors. *"Hey, taller kid, go over there!"*

Besides, I've long since discovered, the best way to prepare anyone for incoming turmoil is to make them think everything is calm until the last second. People work better in overdrive, with nothing but their fight or flight guiding them. The longer they sit with their anxiety, the more it drains them, gives them room for error.

I turn to Beth, who's standing behind me, still as a summer morning, waiting for whatever. "You said there's no tunnel out of here?"

"No. There's not even any windows."

Many shop owners build their stores close to home and pay tunnel builders to connect the two places. That way, the owner can work late and scramble home safely if they stay past nighttime, when the curfew alarms hit. Tunnel building is such a sought-after project now, it costs top dollar to have one dug out, which is another reason why only already-wealthy people own shops.

I rub my eyes. "All right, everyone take a wall and give all the boxes a thorough check. Look for anything that might help us."

Bradley puts a hand on each kid's shoulder, connecting them all into a singular shape. It reminds me of when my mom used to fold up paper and cut little diamonds into the folds. When she opened the paper up, it would make a line of people connected by their hands.

"There's not really much to look at in here," Bradley says.

"You'd be surprised what you can find," I respond.

He accepts this and drags his kids toward the far corner

where four stacks of boxes three high block most of the view. Brayson pulls his dad forward, getting into the idea of searching. Just as I hoped. Distraction.

Beth, too, gets into the search, pushing boxes around, looking for God knows what. I haven't told them what to look for, and to be honest, I have no idea myself. As I explore the front wall, I'm listening out for sounds upstairs, hoping to hear anything, however faint, from the street. It's all very confusing. Alarms in the daytime, beasts out killing unprepared people. This isn't like The Eight. They use the creatures to scare people, not to create havoc. The killing is supposed to be just for those blatantly disregarding curfew. Which can only mean one thing, but I don't want to think about it.

As if reading my next thought, Bradley says, "I don't think they're going to come in here."

He might be right. The beasts don't typically break into places. Otherwise, they'd end up killing innocent people sticking to curfew. But who knows what they were told to do today. The beasts obey above all else.

"Jason, was it?" Beth asks.

I look at her. "Yes."

"Can I speak to you for a second?" She nods up the stairs.

I glance at Bradley, who's glaring right back, suspicion burning through his smiling façade. Beth catches it too and tries to alleviate his concern. "I just don't want to say it in front of the kids."

Bradley huffs and bends down to his children's level. "Take your brother and go to the corner. Stay where I can see you and keep quiet."

He gives Brayson a gentle push, and Brayson grabs his brother's hand, pulling him toward the corner. His eyes grow wide, and he turns back to his dad. "Where are you going?"

I point up. "Just to the top of the stairs. But we aren't

going to open the door. We'll be right there where you can see us."

I lead the way. At the top of the steps, Beth and Bradley squeeze in so we're all fitting on two slender stairs.

For a moment, we're all silent, listening out for any chaos on the other side of the door. Nothing. It's eerily silent.

Beth finally talks, keeping her voice as low as possible, just above a whisper. "At school, kids are always saying crazy stuff, and most of the time, I don't believe it, but with the alarms going off in the daytime, it got me wondering about one of the stories."

Bradley perks up. "What was it?"

She shakes her head, doubting herself. "This kid. He's an idiot, and he was probably making it up, but he says his aunt lived in a small town in Massachusetts, and one day, they got daytime alarms too. Turns out The Eight, for whatever reason, decided to destroy the whole town. Sent the beasts in to kill everyone. Just like that, everyone in town was dead, and that was that."

Bradley frowns. "How would your friend know this happened? If The Eight killed everyone, how would he know?"

I rub at my beard, putting together a full picture, and it makes my stomach turn. There's no way. I have to be wrong. But if I'm being honest, I know I'm not. "We have two options here. Either The Eight dropped the bells just to flex, to remind everyone who owns what around here—send some beasts out, let them kill some folks in the street, and scare the ever-living shit out of everyone else—or they're going scorched Earth on the whole town."

Bradley huffs again. "Well, if those are the only options, I'm voting it's option one. If they were going to kill us all, the beasts would be in here already. Before we came into the basement, I heard them just down the road."

I shake my head. "Nah. Think about it. If they were gonna eliminate us all, they'd probably have most of the beasts at the perimeter of town to make sure we don't escape. And they probably have packs in different areas. The pack we heard has to go into each building and scour the whole place, hunting down anyone in hiding. It'll be a little bit before they'd get here, even if they were just down the road."

Beth says, "But why?"

"Option A or option B, either way, they must have gotten wind of some kind of plan from the townspeople."

Bradley put his hand up. "But that doesn't make sense. One of the biggest rebellion groups of all time formed in this town, and when The Eight discovered them, they didn't destroy the whole place."

I rub my eyes, tired. "The Magaziners, I know. Because The Eight knew the names of everyone involved. They were given every single detail and eliminated the threat one by one. If something is going on now, they probably only have a whiff of it. Since they won't have what they need to contain it, they'll just go full kill mode."

Taking a glance back at his kids, Bradley says, "You sure seem to know a lot about how they operate."

There's no way Bradley and Beth would ever find out who I am, and keeping that secret would smooth the rest of our time together, but I find it important to tell them the truth. I don't know why. "I do know a lot about it. I'll explain, and it'll make you all distrust me, but I think you should know who you're stuck with."

Beth's forehead wrinkles, and Bradley shifts, blocking his kids from my view.

"My father was Elmer Wilder." It's all I need to say.

Beth's jaw drops, and Bradley scoffs.

"You've got to be fucking kidding me." Bradley runs his hands through his hair.

Beth, stuck in a basement and trapped with the son of one of the world's most hated men, still manages to hold on to her heart. "I'm sorry for your loss."

"Don't be. I hated my father. He was never a good man, even before he did what he did. And I know you won't believe me, but I am not my father's son."

Bradley shakes his head, thinking about all the new information. Finally, he sighs. "Listen, I didn't do anything wrong. If I'm trapped down here in some kind of scorched Earth plan like you said, then all I want to do is keep my kids alive. I'm not gonna lie, it's going to be hard to trust you, but even if you're just like your father, I don't see how it affects me or what's happening right now. You could be The Magaziners, The Eight, or totally unaffiliated. It doesn't change my plans to keep us alive. And if you *are* with The Eight, they obviously don't care much for you if you're out here with the beasts on the loose."

Beth leans against the door. "Speaking of, I feel like we should check on the situation out there."

I nod. "Yeah, not a bad idea. Beth and I will go check it out. Bradley, get back to looking for anything down here we can use to our advantage."

He takes a slow step down while remaining faced in our direction. He's untrusting, and I don't blame him, and I can see the thoughts flying through his mind. He doesn't know if he wants to obey my request, but he also doesn't have any better ideas. After dropping a few steps down, he relents. Turns and goes.

I get ahead of Beth and crack the door open. The store looks as normal, and the windows are intact. Outside the windows, the street is empty, with the exception of the crispy corpse lying on the sidewalk across the way. The alarms have long stopped, and the street is eerily quiet, especially for this time of day.

Beth and I creep out but remain behind the counter. Maybe The Eight already called the beasts back. Was this all just a normal drill, done during the day to put fear in the people, keep them on their toes? No. Beth's right. They're going scorched Earth, and I know exactly why. I'm still just refusing to believe it.

Just as I'm about to move around the counter to get a better view of the road, three beasts enter our view. They're standing in the middle of the road, hunched and drooling. Their humanoid faces send a shockwave of terror down my spine. I've never seen one so close. Their eyes are devoid of color, just billiard-sized black abysses. Their mouths hang down like their jaws no longer work, and their teeth drip from their gums in sharp crags.

I quickly duck behind the counter and peek over. The beasts turn their heads left and right, debating on which side to explore next. Beth isn't even trying to scope them out, completely folded into a ball on the floor behind the counter.

Something flashes behind the front windows of Mackey's Hacky Sacks and Outdoor Games, and the beasts take no time in deciding. They charge the building, smashing through the windows. Within seconds, the same man who used the fire extinguisher earlier screams. Even from here, I can see the blood splashing against the remaining shards of window still in place.

"Let's go," I say to Beth, grabbing her hand and pulling her toward the door.

Staying low, she gets to her feet and follows me down the stairs. She closes the door nice and slowly, not making a peep. We fly down the stairs to see Bradley standing in waiting with a smile on his face.

"You're not going to believe this," he says as he points to a section of wall exposed. They'd moved a few piles of boxes and revealed a carved-out section of wall. A tunnel.

"Holy shit," I say.

Bradley walks side-by-side with me, a little too close for my liking. I touch my phone, a slight comfort in the madness.

"Yeah, Finn was checking boxes and said, 'Dad, the wall is different behind here.' So, I came over and moved the boxes. It was just a flimsy piece of wood over the hole. I don't have a flashlight, and the one on my phone doesn't go very far in, so I have no idea how far it goes or *where* it goes, but it's something."

I move over to the hole. Everyone surrounds it now. "Okay, so everyone go in one after the other. I'll go last and put the boxes back as close and possible, and then I'll slide the wood back over the hole. It won't keep our secret for long, but it could slow the beasts down."

"Where do you think it goes?" Brayson asks.

"My guess is Willow's house."

"Who's Willow?" Finn asks.

"I assume it's who owns Willow's Ice Cream."

Beth nods. "Willow Fielder."

I turn to her. My next question doesn't matter, but I want to know. "But who owns it?"

She furrows her brow. "Willow Fielder."

"No, I mean which one of The Eight."

People don't own businesses by their lonesome. They have to share the ownership with one of The Eight.

Beth stutters. "I guess I don't know. Never thought to ask."

She's telling the truth, I can tell. And why would a teenage kid give a shit? Why do I?

"We better go. The beasts were across the street. It won't take them long to clear that building out, and then they'll be here."

The boys' faces turn cold, eyes growing wide and welling

up with tears of terror. I give Bradley a tap, indicating he should go first.

He stops dead before the hole. "I don't think you should come with us." He turns back to me but keeps his head aimed at the hole, unable to look at me. He knows he's condemning me to death.

"I don't really care what you think," I say.

Now he moves his head, putting his eyes right in front of mine. A steel grin made from gritting his teeth slides across his face. "Fine. But I'm getting my kids out of this. And I will kill you if you get in the way. I couldn't place why it bothered me so much when you mentioned who your father was. Obviously, you're not working for The Eight, or they wouldn't have left you out here with the beasts. It's not like those things will discern your relationship with the companies before ripping your throat out. They only eat. Politics is of no concern to them."

"And you're exactly right about that."

"But then I remembered your father didn't work for The Eight either. He was just a weasel who ratted out the best chance we had at freedom from them. And then The Magaziners had him killed for being a traitor. Makes me wonder if you have a bone to pick with the resistance. And maybe just like your father, you'd rat the people out to get in The Eight's good graces. Sure, I'm not part of any resistance, but if I plan to escape their fire and brimstone, you might just want to inform them of our plans. I promise you, if you do, I will kill you."

"Good speech. Let's go," is all I offer. I have plenty to say, but we don't have the time for it. If this asshole plans to keep his kids alive, he should learn not to monologue.

And as if on cue, a window smashes above us.

GO!" I yell.

Beth doesn't wait for Bradley and dives into the hole. She scurries into the darkness on her hands and knees. Bradley finally makes his move, and his kids trail behind, jumping into the thick black of the unknown. I try to move the piles of boxes back into place slowly, so as not to make too loud of a scraping noise against the cement floor, but I'm terrified. I can hear the clicking of sharp nails landing on the tiling above my head.

Once the boxes sufficiently cover the hole, I grip the wooden slat and slide it over the hole, draping myself in complete darkness. Just as I finish, the basement door smashes, and the sound of its pieces raining down the steps is enough to send me crawling with all of my might.

The tunnel is big enough for me to turn with ease but small enough that we couldn't dodge the beasts if they make their way in. And they will. The beasts operate on smell and know when humans are close. They'll find us; I have no doubt. It's only a matter of when. My only hope is that when the beasts catch me, I'll get to hold my phone for a few seconds before I die.

As far away from the tunnel entrance as I am, I can still hear the beasts slashing away at boxes. They're nothing if not thorough.

"Faster," I whisper to the crowd in front of me. They're slowing me down.

We reach a turn in the tunnel, and the walls close in. The further we move, the thinner the tunnel gets. Then I smell something. I can't place it, and its fairly faint. Maybe Beth wore perfume, and I'm just getting a whiff.

As we squeeze in to the next turn, my anxiety needles up a notch. I don't like enclosed spaces much. I wouldn't call it a phobia, but when things start getting this tight and maneuvering gets this difficult, yeah, maybe it's a phobia.

The sound of the wood board crashing apart echoes through the cavernous chamber. It's a new form of alarm but not without the same foreboding and shock of the one on the streets. Then comes the sound of the beasts' hands and feet. Their sharpened claws make a tick-tack sound as they run.

"Move," I scream. Dear God, we're trapped in here with these things. Nowhere to run, nowhere to shift even. We can't face our deaths head-on. It's barreling from behind, and the beasts will tear us to shreds without so much as seeing our eyes.

The boys have lost their ability to hold in their sounds. One of them screams in fear. I hear the line of heavy breathing in front of me, the panic coming out in hyperventilation.

As we crawl faster and faster, the space makes it more and more difficult. It's getting so tight, I wonder if this tunnel is even finished, if we're crawling toward a dead end. I feel the walls squeezing into my shoulders, which are pushing into my body.

The smell is getting stronger too. A deep floral smell like a grandmother's perfume. It's enough to make me choke.

Behind me, a beast snarls. It's so damn close. The line in front of me collapses. Beth falls on her face, causing Bradley and his sons to do the same. Like a comical chain reaction, everyone stumbles over the person before them until I, too, fall face-first into the heel of Brayson's shoe.

I clench, knowing that this slowdown will give the beasts all the time they need to reach me. I'm dead, and I can't die. Not yet. With the little room I have, I reach for my phone and bring it to my face. As the light comes on, I see I have 37 missed calls and even more unread texts. I enter my password, and the home screen comes to life.

The texts are from different numbers, and each one

contains nothing more than a series of numbers and letters. With the little room I have, I chance a look behind me. It takes effort to find a position where my head can turn. I just need to know how many seconds I have, but trying to look backwards is taking them away. I know it, but again, I fight myself.

What I see is so incredible, I have to laugh. Two beast heads wriggle and battle each other for positioning, both stuck in the ever-tightening tunnel. It reminds of *The Three Stooges*. My father, who spent his life being a prick, a militant, angry parent, loved the Stooges. I grew to love them too because they represented the only time my house held peace. When the Stooges got my father laughing, it meant I might not catch a beating for a few hours.

He said the whippings happened for my own good, to toughen me up for the inevitable war. A war he waged, he prepared for. He built armies, created rules and laws, and from his harsh breath, an uprising bloomed like baking bread. And after all that, all the lectures and planning and ranting and teaching me with fists and belts, after all of it, he sold himself out and gave everything to The Eight.

I laugh so hard at the stuck beasts that I can't tell when it becomes crying, but it does. I look back at the posse in front of me, and they're all still, all turned to watch me unfold and rip apart.

I sniffle and wipe away the tears. "They're stuck. They can't reach us."

And then it hits me. The smell. It was all on purpose. The size of the tunnel shrank so someone, probably Willow, could navigate through it but the beasts couldn't. But the beasts can speak to each other through their minds and, with their power of smell, could inform other beasts where their prey were heading. Unless Willow put something in the tunnel to fuck up their scent.

I had presumed we were heading toward Willow's house, but now I'm seeing a bigger picture. Willow has secrets. I want to know more.

"Let's keep going," I say. "Eventually, those fuckers will squeeze their way through."

The line goes back to crawling, but the sense of urgency diminishes. They're moving slower, which is probably wise. Who knows what lays ahead. Maybe Willow planned traps for the beasts.

As we move forward, I think about my father. I'll go to my grave never knowing why he gave up The Magaziners. A group formed from his own words, molded by his vision. His whole life, he railed against The Eight. He blamed them for every problem we faced, every bad day, every character flaw. "Do you see what they do to me?" he'd shout as the only form of apology we'd ever get for his explosive abuse. So why did he sell them out just before they could have succeeded?

I never hated Joe Rancone for killing my father in the diner that day. I hated him for exposing my father. Had he not done what he'd done, the news would have never released that he was the traitor to the resistance. Since Joe took away the place to aim their rage, the people focused it on me instead. New beatings, bullying, and pain. I wish I could have killed my father myself.

I came up with fantastical explanations for why he would sell himself out. Maybe The Eight caught him and threatened to kill me if he didn't expose the organization. But I knew that was false because my father loved his hate for The Eight far more than he ever loved me.

That's the problem with hate. It becomes a part of you, and when you spend all your time with it, you marry it. For better or worse, till death do you part. I know this because I hold a brick ton of it inside me. It festers in there, brewing and bubbling, waiting for a detonation.

The further we move toward our unknown futures, the softer the beast's growls become. They can't reach us. Up ahead, the line dead halts, and Beth lets out an "Oof."

"What happened?" I ask.

"This is it. I hit a wall."

Please, God, tell me there's a way out. If this turns out to be a dead-end tunnel, if my original concern of it being unfinished was spot on, we are absolutely fucked. Just turning around is nearly impossible, and even if we pull it off, the beasts will be right there stuck in our way, blocking us from getting out.

"Feel around. Is there anything above you?"

I hear the pitter-patter of palms on stone as everyone feels all around them.

"Got something," Beth says. "There's wood above me."

"Does it open? Can you move it?"

She grunts, huffs, struggles. Something thunks, and a low light enters the cave. I feel the light enter me like air, opening my lungs.

"Oh, thank God," I say.

Bradley laughs and the boys giggle. It's nice to hear. Relief. Within the depths of emotion, the total range of feeling, I forgot all about relief. I think the world did too.

The rocky ceiling is carved out a foot or so up, and the wood lay on top of a hole. Beth shifts it over and worms her body around to give herself leeway to climb up. I wait to see if she screams up there before giving the boys the go-ahead to follow. Once they're both up, Bradley goes, giving me a little nod on the way. His way of saying we're all good.

I climb up last. We're in a small room, probably about 30 feet by 30 feet, and it's all wood. Floors, walls, and flat ceiling. This is definitely not Willow's house. More like her shed if anything. The room is barely lit; only the last slivers of daylight creeping in through a window give it any texture, and it's that muted light that came into the tunnel when Beth opened the wood panel. My vision coalesces with the layout, and I nearly dive back into the hole at the sight of something moving by the window. I realize quickly, though, that's it's just an old woman sitting in a rocking chair. If she's turned to recognize us, it happened before I got up here.

I look at Beth, hoping she knows what I'm asking with my eyes. *Is this Willow?* She understands and nods. We all stand behind the woman in an arch, no one moving, no one talking. But every individual breath makes its own song.

The woman speaks. "The Eight don't pay attention to the woods. I made this place, jeez, had to be ten years ago now. I just wanted somewhere away from their watchful eye."

Something is shimmering outside the window. I presumed it was the last vestiges of sun crawling behind the tree line, but then I see it's more volatile than that. I move closer. It's fire.

"Jesus, they set those buildings on fire? Weren't the beasts enough?"

The woman laughs. "They didn't do that. The people did. Decided in the last seconds of their life that they wouldn't sell their souls too. They'd dictate how they go out."

Her words remind me of the man who set himself on fire just a short while ago. *They already had my soul. Might as well have the body too.*

The view proves the shelter is on top of a hill. I can't catch my bearings because I don't remember ever ascending while in the tunnels. But I guess that's how life works. Sometimes it all moves so subtly you hardly notice it. Who was the first to recognize when we were all *falling*?

The view is amazing, though. I can see the whole town, all of main street, the Pawcatuck flowing around it all. I see the mill. And I see, a little farther away, safe from all of the violence, the Sand Rock Alliance Corporation headquarters.

"You'll notice one set of buildings is nice and safe, though," Bradley says.

The woman laughs. "Always." And then, "Motherfuckers."

"Which one owned your ice cream shop?" I ask, unsure why I care so much to have asked this question twice now.

She points to the ominous brutalist stronghold in the distance. "Figured I'd go with the home team."

"Makes sense," I say.

A squeak leaves her throat, and she covers her face. I leave her to it. A few seconds later, she wipes her cheeks and says, "I just wanted to live. You know?"

Beth comes to Willow's side and puts her hand on top of the old woman's arm. "I really loved working for you."

A branch snaps outside the shed, and then another. I spin my head back toward the window and see them. Beasts. Dozens.

The woman stands up and sighs. She pulls the bottom of her shirt, neatening it. "Well, they're here now. This is it."

I brace for impact, waiting for the beasts to barge in. The old woman holds up a contraption and clicks a button. The ground outside explodes in small bursts. Dirt flies in the air, creating a dust storm. Within it, blood and guts. She'd rigged the entire grounds in preparation for this. I'm impressed.

"Holy shit," Bradley says before laughing.

Willow sighs. "There'll be a second wave shortly. Just figured I'd wipe out as many as I could before I go. I wasn't expecting company if this sort of thing ever happened, but I'm glad to know I'll go out giving y'all some time to escape."

Beth puts her hand on the woman's shoulder. "Come on. Let's go."

"I don't have running in me, dear."

I'm not waiting for this argument to unfold, so I head right for the door. It creaks open, and the cool evening air hits my face. As I step into the woods, Bradley and the boys come charging in right behind me.

I move to the front of the house, where pieces of the beasts speckle the ground. It's a beautiful sight, but I'm more interested in the view.

"Where are we going?" Bradley asks.

Beth runs out from the house and joins us. "She's refusing to come with us. Where do we go now?"

"That's what I just asked." Bradley snaps his finger in front of my face as I stare out at the town. "Come back to us, Jason. Where do we go?"

I look over at him. He has blue eyes. I hadn't noticed before. They're the color of a well-chlorinated pool. I look down at his children. They both have bowl cuts. The older one has mismatched teeth where the adult ones have grown in next to the baby ones. Weird gaps and varying sizes. The younger one, was it Finn? Anyway, he's got freckles.

Lastly, I look at Beth. She's still, even now, holding hope in her gaze.

"Thank you," I say to her.

"For what?"

"Being the better of us."

Bradley taps my arm. "We have to go, Jason."

In the distance, twigs crunch. The second wave is coming, just like Willow assured.

"I'm sorry," I say to Bradley.

I slide my phone out of my pocket. I could have done this in the ice cream shop, in the basement, the tunnel; I had so many chances, and now it's probably too late. But this was never about anything other than myself, and I refused to deprive myself of a view. Jeez, I just wanted the cement ledge by the Pawcatuck. How could I have known such a splendid one would fall into my lap.

The crunching grows louder. Bradley pulls at my shirt

before giving up. He and the kids sprint off. Beth stays and watches me.

I go to the group text and hit the code. Q45FP-9.

People will know what I did today. It'll be whispered for years to come. They'll assign a method to my madness and a reason for my actions, and they'll be wrong.

Boom.

Tanner's Mill explodes. It's powerful and loud, and even all the way up here, the ground shakes.

I didn't do this for the resistance.

Boom.

The entire town square lights up in a fiery ball of orange and red. Waves of tendrilled heat reach for the sky. Beth covers her face and screams.

I didn't do this for The Eight.

Boom.

The Sand Rock Alliance Corporation headquarters evaporates. Explosions after explosions collapse each brutalist building one after the other. The sound is so strong it shakes the trees around us.

It'll do nothing. All I did was kill a bunch of innocent workers. Sand Rock will bounce back, and with the other seven companies, they'll strengthen their security and use the attack as an excuse for girding our freedoms even tighter.

More folks will suffer for this.

Boom.

The neighborhoods blast into flames. All the houses disintegrate. Beth screams. Her family probably lived in one of those.

The Eight had gotten wind of my plans, knew I had intentions of destroying their headquarters, and in response, they planned to destroy the entire town. Unbeknownst to them, I planned to do the same. It wouldn't work to destroy some buildings. I needed to wipe out their entire stronghold, their home base. If they killed the people, it was a response, a way to let the people know who was in control. If I killed the people, it was a message. It says to every future conspirator, "We can own them as they own us." I didn't know I'd be stopping their scorched Earth plans tonight, but it's an added delight. We both destroyed the same target, but my actions lead to chaos in place of their control.

There's nothing noble in the destruction. Raised by abuse, forced to accept a mission I hadn't understood. My whole life was one wasted missive after the next. And after a lifetime of being fed a villain-in-the-distance from a villain in my face, it all disappeared. Washed away. My father made me his bomb and clipped me of my wick.

And this?

Boom.

I feel the heat from behind me as the hills explode. Beth turns, wide-eyed, and screams anew. Bradley and his children just went that way.

All this just to say, "Fuck you," to my father. *You don't get to betray the mission. You made my whole identity the resistance. If you won't finish the fucking thing, I will. Even if we all lose in the end.*

I turn and see Willow in the window, staring at me wide-eyed and mouth agape. The fire catches the back of her shed. In a few moments, she'll be dead.

The beasts break through the tree line, three of them. They charge Beth and I, but she isn't even paying attention, her back turned to them, seeing the flames up the hill encroach on us.

See me. See me now, you motherfuckers.

Before long, the beasts rip into me. The pain is unbearable. Yet, I hardly feel a thing.

I built the revival of The Magaziners.

A lifetime wasted, weighed down by beatings and lectures,

only to have the man handing me those beatings and lectures betray his own tenets. It killed me.

A beast clenches my neck and bites. "Fuck you, Dad. I finished it, you fucking traitor," are the words I can't say because my throat is shredded through.

We are all bombs. Heroes just don't detonate like the rest of us.

EDMUND KEMPER

"One side of me says, 'I'd like to talk to her, date her.' The other side me says, 'I wonder what her head would look like on a stick.'"

—Edmund Kemper

ZEMBLANITY

BY ERIN BANKS

She had taken the job at the pediatric dentist's because she loved hurting children.

Of course, she wouldn't dispute that adults experienced agonizing physical pain in the same manner, but there was something more perversely holistic about hurting a child in that, along with it, one always destroyed a part of their faith in people, safety, justice.

She could see it in the way their eyes first flew open and then squinted in an attempt at being brave before almost immediately breaking. It was more than their eyes that broke, however; it was their very spirit welling up inside them and spilling over to form a steady river down the reddened blotches on their cherub cheeks.

They left the practice a little emptier, a little less themselves than nature intended. And upon their return, they had already adopted the fearful posture of a beaten dog. Rinse and repeat.

There were three secrets to staying in employment. The first was to content herself with what she could have rather than what she'd like to have. Children were little snitches, be it verbally or nonverbally, thus obviously, she couldn't ram the drill through their tongues whilst cackling like a maniac. But she could drill too deeply, pinch a nerve, aggravate a wound, and all of this even with the clueless parents present.

The second secret involved scattering. She had her favorites but ought not to hurt them with great frequency lest their parents eventually take them to another dentist, only to discover that none of the procedures should actually have caused discomfort of this magnitude.

Thus, she didn't select specific victims but specific procedures because should questions arise or the medical board be alerted, she could either blame it on outdated tools or, should all else fail, admit she simply lacked the skillset to perform procedure X painlessly.

Of course, this was the ideal, and she herself had recently been escalating.

The third secret was simply the biological reality that she was a woman, and women could get away with almost anything. On the rare account they didn't, they received far lighter sentences.

And yet, she was utterly incapable of determining why she was a pedosadist. None of what she did aroused her. But she enjoyed it; it was a heart arousal, she surmised.

Along with it, however, she cherished the emotional contentment of helping someone in need, rescuing spiders and other creepy-crawlies that found their way into her bungalow, and her heart broke for every death reported on the news—even children's. Put a child in front of her, though, and . . .

She had never suffered a traumatic brain or head injury, had not been abused or neglected, and yet she suffered this harrowing affliction whose impulses she found more and more difficult to curb.

Suffer! one may exclaim in disbelief. Indeed, she suffered from actual and terrible guilt as soon as she closed the front door, uttering the oft-repeated promise never to harm a child again.

She had grasped at straws over the years, going as far as pondering whether it was, perhaps, her name that had some subconscious psychological effect on her.

Eliza Payne.

She was neither popular nor shunned in school, but some of the boys teasingly referred to her as Elicit Pain.

"What's in a name?" Perhaps Shakespeare was less of a poet than a psychologist without a degree; who knows?

Her guilt and shame were real. Eliza forsook earthly pleasures—food, intimacy, vacations, anything—in an attempt to rein herself in. If she did well and abstained from harm, she allowed herself a treat. Alas, she had never earned one in her twenty-five years on this planet.

She hated herself for what she did, at least within the confinements of her eggshell walls, amid her tastefully chosen decor, and cried herself to sleep on a nightly basis. But with the first ring of her alarm clock, she already looked forward to doing it again, last night's vow swiftly abandoned.

At one point, she wanted to do the right thing and kill herself yet found herself incapable of going through with it on the grounds that she was staunchly agnostic. She couldn't be sure there was a hell and that eternal torment awaited her.

***

As a boy, he had dreamt of being somebody but could never stick with any one dream. At first, he blamed the limitedness of human years for contributing to his anxious scatteredness, until, that is, he identified women as the root issue of all his woes.

He started out wanting to be a wrestler, but his height and

lack of fitness posed a challenge. So he tried to make light of that fact and used self-deprecating humor to try and weasel his way into the cool kids club.

But soon, everyone ignored his ironically chosen wrestling moniker of *Goliath* and started calling him *The Comedian*. It was funny at first, then swiftly devolved into bullying, and as a consequence, he decided to turn his back on this his first life's dream, seeking refuge in standup comedy instead.

As a wrestler, however, he hadn't been alone in the ring. He'd played off of others and had to focus on the steps to get to the choreographed ending, meaning he had never had time to notice his anxiety.

As a standup comedian, he stared back at the crowd staring at him and froze in awkward terror.

That was when he had a bolt of inspiration that acting classes might help, and he packed his bags to move his life from Kitchener to Washington on a student visa. He hadn't been too shabby but ultimately dropped out because of the way that tall giraffe Emily had raised her chin to look down on him after he had mustered up the courage to ask her out. Clearly, the prerogative was to emphasize he was three inches shorter than her.

"Whilst I thank you for your flattering offer, I must regretfully decline, being that I'm not available," were her words.

He recalled them as if they were being spoken to him right then and there whenever he thought of the experience, and each time, he was overcome with homicidal rage, remembering with embarrassment the angry wank he'd had that night.

His phone carefully shielded by cellophane, he stared at the photo he had secretly snapped of her. But while relieving himself all over her faux angelic smile, he'd already started crying because in his mind's eye, he saw her penetrating blue eyes narrow, nose wrinkle, and lips curl up in disgust over what he was doing. Thus he packed up and returned to Kitchener to resume his old job at the gas station near Cherry Hills.

Working the cash register and restocking shelves, brewing coffee, wiping counters, he seethed inside, obsessing over how everything he had ever done, all his grand aspirations, in truth only cloaked vulnerable hopes of girls taking an interest in him.

School had taught him that girls liked funny guys. But he wasn't the tall, witty stud to make them swoon; he was the fat little clown to comfort them while the tall, witty studs kept breaking their hearts over and over, one by one.

And while the other wrestlers, standup comedians, and actors always had droves of women throwing themselves at them after shows and classes, he got out his water bottle and suckled on the short straw while imagining it was the tit of one of the tramps who called him "bro."

They had made him impotent. Kind of. He could only fantasize about girls who had rejected him or whom he knew would reject him, the shame, rejection, pain, and anger, rolled into one, having a seemingly irreversible physiological effect on him.

The only girl he had ever been with was a girl from Southeast Asia that he met online. Had he targeted Asia specifically? Maybe subconsciously.

For Seresa Baccay, he knew, he would finally fulfill all of the criteria which women—half-sentient flesh around stingy holes—had: he was taller than her, he was funny, he was a provider, and he was faithful. He was faithful because he had no other options, of course.

They had exchanged photos and voice notes via the app, and yet there were many things photos could not convey. He had always loved Seresa's smile, but seeing her in person, he realized it was always plastered across her face despite her eyes remaining untouched by it.

The fact that she still took him home with her from the airport in spite of the side glances she threw at him meant she wanted that green card bad. And he wanted to finally know what it was like to fuck at age thirty-five.

Begrudgingly, he tried to accept his fate of having to settle for a transactional relationship, but Seresa did not hold up her end of the bargain.

He couldn't elicit one single moan or pelvic thrust from that woman, no matter how hard he tried, and the way she still always politely smiled and patronizingly patted him on the shoulder each time he lifted himself up on his elbows to look at her killed his erection.

And she giggled.

She had the audacity to giggle!

It was the cherry on top of the ice cream sundae of shit that was his life, and in a knee-jerk reaction, he slapped Seresa across the face with so much gusto her head flew to the side. She shrieked, protectively covering her whole head with her arm.

There was something about her fright and pain that let the blood rush back into his loins so rapidly that for a split second, he thought he was going to explode right then and there.

He couldn't tell what made him do it because he'd never had that type of fantasy before, but he then wrapped his hands around Seresa's throat and started to choke her. Finally, her body moved underneath him, spasming to and fro against his, as she kept mouthing his name.

"Billy. Billy, please."

But it wasn't the fear itself, in the classic sense, that led to his release, more what it represented. In her fear, she finally acknowledged that he was someone, an individual human being instead of the means to an end. For the first time, he did not fulfill a purpose for a woman, and the experience was exhilarating.

He had agency. He would not be humiliated any longer because he had the power to prevent it. Drunk on the cognition that he deserved respect but would have its shadow-twin fear instead if that was all he could have, he laughed maniacally, not even making it to the third stroke before climaxing as Seresa sobbed beneath him and, for the first time in his life, he did not.

She didn't marry him for the green card after the incident but at least didn't go to the police or get him reported. The rest of his stay, he changed hostels after each time he had taken a sex worker to his room to strangle her in order to get off, now that he knew he even could in the presence of a woman.

Without Seresa, he doubted he would have become a serial killer. He sometimes daydreamed about flying back to see her, to confess, and each time, that fantasy ended differently.

Sometimes, she wept and apologized to him, promising to love and never abandon him again, and they lived a quiet island life together.

Other times, her apology riled him in his self-invoked visions. Her promise rang fake in his ears, and he killed her for doing this to him in the first place.

His facial muscles and fingers twitched as he envisioned taking a knife and flaying her, feeding her the animated, bloody piece of meat that was her own skin until she threw up, and laughing when he got to the part when he sliced off her titties, stuffing them down her throat and hacking off her fingers to shove them up her fucking cunt.

Afterwards, though, he cried, hands covering his face, both in the fantasy as well as in real life, because he didn't really want to kill her. He hadn't actually wanted to kill anyone, but where did they think all that rejected love would go? How would it not eventually have spoiled and mutated into murder!?

***

Eliza had never had an interest in serial killers whatsoever until she read about what news outlets had dubbed the Waterloo Wrangler, due to disposing of the bodies of his victims with a lasso around their necks. Living in Waterloo herself, she had sporadically followed the case out of a sense of thoughtless self-preservation.

One day, she was waiting in line at the grocery store when her gaze fell upon one of the newspapers with the headline "Waterloo Wrangler: Who Is He? Psychologist Reveals All."

They'd gone all out, interviewing a renowned Californian psychologist rather than a local one for the purpose. Flipping to the article, the highlighted quote read that the tears discovered on the bodies weren't the victims' but strongly presumed to be the killer's. The victims showed signs of having been held for a while, wearing fresh new clothes, being fed and hydrated, but also having lacerations around their wrists and ankles. The last two had had bite marks; the last one was missing strips of skin that had already started to scab. The killer was escalating.

No sooner than Eliza saw the psychologist's cautious profile of the offender did the most outlandish idea pop into her head. So fantastical was it that it had to be divine intuition, possibly even intervention.

How do you catch a serial killer?

Or rather, how do you catch a serial killer as a laywoman without any background in law enforcement? You use his profile against him.

At least, that was Eliza's theory. And hope.

***

Billy roared every cuss word known to man at his laptop screen, grabbing the sides of it with both hands and shaking it. It was really the host of that new channel he wanted to throttle. His night was ruined.

Over the last handful of months, he'd gotten used to falling asleep with a sheepish grin on his face, male appendage still in hand, because he was finally being paid his dues. He had it all, fear-respect and love-attention. When the first Waterloo Wrangler pages and groups started sprouting up on social media, he couldn't believe his eyes.

These girls didn't even know what he looked like yet gathered to share AI-generated pictures of themselves together with how they envisioned Billy, the results not seldom resembling romance book covers. They went as far as writing fan fiction about him, and there was even a group with the name "Waterloo Wrangler Haiku Society."

Night after night, he returned home grateful his fans made him forget he was still Billy Shupert, the loser who worked the same gas station job he'd had in high school. Perusing these groups turned from hobby to obsession fast, and he blamed them for the body count he was racking up, for their members required content to remember to love him.

Again, he was left having to work to be loved. Regardless of what he did, it was never enough. It was not enough that he simply existed. Even his fellowship's love turned out to be conditional, transactional.

But then that video popped up.
The girl had named her channel "The Waterloo *Weakling*."

His heart thumped in his chest as soon as his eyes stumbled across the last word.

Even worse than the name was the smug grin she wore on her hideous face while presenting "his case." She took everything that psychologist had said about him and twisted it. He'd kept the article, oft-quoted by the media and on social media, and carried it around in his wallet, occasionally tracing his thumb across it to remind himself that there was at least one person who had seen into his soul without recoiling in disgust. He hadn't gotten all his facts right, not his motivations, but where Dr. Yeoman empathized, she mocked. Where Dr. Yeoman found tactful words, she denigrated. Where Dr. Yeoman referred to him as someone whose mind had come to the wrong conclusions, she called him an impotent misogynist.

She had gone as far as being belligerent about the type of knot he tied around his victims' necks, accusing him of being too stupid to tie a noose, resulting in the lasso type rope with its sliding knot instead. More than hating her, he hated the fact that she was right. He couldn't even tie a noose correctly. But it bothered him that she somehow knew and dared provoke him in that manner.

He giggled like an imp at the average Joe and plain Jane making hateful assumptions about him because they were lacking in depth, psychological understanding, and reality. This girl . . . this girl was different. She made him feel like the fat little clown with acne inversa and hyperhidrosis, too gross to do more than glance at, let alone touch, again.

And that's when he knew.

This would be his legacy before killing himself.

He would find her.

And he would obliterate her before taking his own life.

He would leave a note. No, a manifesto. Yes, yes, a manifesto about why women such as Eliza died at the hand of serial killers.

He would clearly lay out how they were to blame and could have prevented their own deaths. Perhaps Dr. Yeoman would narrate a documentary about him . . . perhaps he himself could even watch from the afterlife, Billy mused.

The "Waterloo Weakling" channel had been around for no more than two weeks yet was already filled with nearly twice as many videos.

It was almost as though she were begging to be noticed; though, he thought to himself, certainly not by him. It would be the surprise of her young life.

Not only did Eliza Payne introduce herself by name at the start of each video, she also walked around her home and even openly walked out her front and back doors to sit down on the wrap-around porch, thus giving him a good glimpse of the street with all its surrounding homes. In one shot, he could make out a street sign at the corner further down the road.

He had her.

***

It was a tad amusing how he was traipsing around the living room after sneaking inside through the glass sliding door Eliza had specifically left open for the Waterloo Wrangler. Truth be told, she was a tad disappointed it had taken him this long to locate her.

He was apparently convinced she couldn't see him out of the corner of her eye.

Moreover, he was not a light breather, and although she wouldn't turn her head just yet, she could already tell he was overweight due to his suppressed asthmatic wheezes. The faint smell of old cigarette smoke filled her home, and she knew that even if she closed her eyes, she would be able to tell where he was in proximity to her.

One of his bones, likely his knee, popped as he walked up the staircase behind her, and now her curiosity was raised. Did he intend to search the whole home in order to ascertain she was indeed alone?

She had played this moment through so often in her mind, but it had never lost its potency. She was prepared for anything and everything under the sun, or so she believed.

And so Eliza waited a while.

And waited.

And waited.

But he wouldn't return, and she realized she now had to search her own home for him. Letting her nose lead her, she swiftly determined he was hiding in her bedroom closet.

Ah. He liked the classics.

"Hello!" she called towards the closet. "I know you're in there. I also know you are the Waterloo Wrangler. I had hoped you'd come." She cleared her throat. "My videos were my way of extending an invitation to you, sir."

The door opened, and he stepped out, lasso in hand, ready to pounce. Instead, he merely said, "Oh," when he laid eyes on the gun Eliza's fingers were tightly wound around. His shoulders slumped. He resembled one of the children Eliza had broken, like a dog with its tail tucked between its hind legs, and she was stirred to want to give him a hug.

"First of all, I'd like to apologize for the content of the videos. Truth be told, I believe none of it, but you can't argue they didn't serve their purpose."

She paused once more, finding it difficult to breathe from the anticipation.

"I have a proposal for you, sir."

Billy cocked his head. He did like how she kept calling

him sir, though his thoughts were racing, his paranoia spiraling out of control. Still, he listened.

"I think I understand you. You didn't really want to kill anyone at all? You were originally looking for a mate, weren't you?"

Billy inhaled sharply, feeling himself blush like a schoolboy. Not even the psychologist had grasped this about him. Could it be . . . could it be . . .? He dared not finish that thought.

"I think we can help each other. I am not so unlike you," she continued. "I can't stop hurting children, and you can't stop hurting women."

She swallowed. "I am offering myself to you. If I willingly stayed with you as your loyal companion," she started up again, her voice even more firm yet oddly enticing, "all I ask in return is that if the urge to kill strikes you, you come to me instead. Torture me, but do not kill. Let me save your life, that of however many women you may still have killed, and however many children I would still have hurt."

Billy blinked. He knew all the individual words she was speaking, could even understand their meaning in context, although he wasn't entirely sure what to make of her quasi-spiritual babble and suspected an ulterior motive he could not yet discern. The prospect of having someone give themselves over to him willingly, however, weighed even harder than the thought that this, too, was essentially a transactional relationship. So tempting was it that he now thought perhaps all relationships were transactional after all.

Still, he asked, "Who wants to be tortured and kept in a hidden basement with no way to escape?" He eyed her gun again. "Are you a cop?"

"No. Here." She held the weapon out to him. "Take it. And then, I beg you, take me."

He took it and guffawed. "You're crazy," he whispered,

half impressed. "You're fucking crazy. Why not kill yourself if you're so desperate? Why not turn yourself in?" His tone was more casual than he felt.

"I could ask you the same question," she promptly retorted, as though aware of his earlier plan to commit suicide after one last hoorah. "I know I deserve hell. What if it does not exist, though? Then I must create the hell on Earth I created for others for myself as well. I believe that is all the atoning a person could do."

It sounded deranged and yet made perfect sense to him.

***

Whistling a tune after he'd restrained and bid Eliza good-night, Billy turned to leave, sliding the wall that hid his sound-proof holding cell in place. He imagined how she would greet him in the morning and what their shared life would be like as he hobbled up the basement steps. It was a macabre story of love and redemption for the ages, testament to *omnia vincit amor;* that, he did not doubt.

On his way to the couch, he leapt in the air and clicked his heels together as he so often had as a boy. He felt like that boy again. That boy filled with hope and endless wonder rather than just hatred and tragedy.

He plopped down on the couch in the front room but winced when Eliza's gun broke his fall. Instinctively, he jumped to his feet, yanking the weapon out of the back of his pants just as the front door came crashing down and the SWAT team opened fire.

Downstairs, Eliza sat down on the bed, neatly folding her cuffed hands, rejoicing at the lives, the souls she had saved.

RICHARD KUKLINSKI

"WHEN I WAS A YOUNG MAN, I FOUND OUT THAT IF YOU hurt somebody bad enough, they'll leave you alone."

—RICHARD KUKLINSKI, the Iceman Killer

DUALITY

BY AJ BROWN

A RAINY DAY TURNED INTO A RAINY NIGHT. ERIK SAT AT the bus stop, his head down, hands in his lap, eyes focused on nothing. People came and went. They stood close enough to the bus stop for the driver to see them and stop, but far enough away so he wouldn't be inclined to talk to them. The lone person who sat beside him was a drunken old man who smelled like cheap whiskey, body odor, and piss. His chin sat on his chest, his gray beard spread out like hairy angel wings. His hair was soaked and matted from the rain, as were his clothes. Like Erik, his hands sat between his legs. Unlike Erik, his eyes were closed.

The busses came. The busses went.

"Hey, buddy," the driver of the last bus of the day said.

Erik looked up. The door was open, and the driver, a big guy who probably had a diabetic issue or was on the verge of it, stared out at him. His hand was on the door lever. Eyes layered with fat lids, puffy bags, and crow's feet wrinkles looked out at him, but Erik said nothing.

"Last ride," the driver called. "You going to sit there or get on?"

Erik licked his lips, nodded, and stood. He walked to the edge of the sidewalk.

"What about your buddy?" the driver asked and jerked his head toward the old man who now sat alone on the bench.

Erik looked back, then turned to the driver. "He's not my buddy. I don't know him."

"How long's he been sitting there like that?"

"All day."

"He looks dead."

Erik shrugged, got on the bus, and put a dollar in the change box. The driver pressed a lever on the side, and the dollar disappeared into a black hole that swallowed money and tokens alike. As he made his way to the back of the bus, Erik glanced out the window at the old man. He shook his head, sat in one of the blue plastic seats on the next to last row, and closed his eyes.

When he opened them, his head leaned against the window. He caught his reflection out the corner of his eye, then straightened. The image in the window was nothing more than a transparent view of a man he thought he knew but wasn't too sure. Erik frowned. He licked his lips.

"I know you," he whispered.

"Better than you think," the man in the window whispered back. That man smiled, showing off a gap on the bottom left row of teeth.

An uneasy feeling crept over Erik. He looked away. A few seconds passed, and he turned his head enough so he could see out the corner of one eye. The transparent man was still there, still looking at Erik with his odd smile.

The bus came to a stop with a sudden jerk. The brakes hissed, and in the sodium arc lights outside, Erik saw smoke billowing up from the back. The side door, near the center and on the right, opened with another loud hiss. Cool air rushed in. The pitter-patter of rain could be heard as it splattered the steps leading out.

"End of the line," the bus driver said. He stood halfway between the front of the bus and the open side door.

Erik nodded. Before he stood, he looked back in the window. The image's eyes were wide and wild. A hyena's smile lined his face. Erik stood. The man followed. The bus driver made his way back to the front of the bus.

Erik went to the front of the bus. He licked his lips again and said, "Have a good night."

The bus driver regarded him with a cautious stare.

Erik stepped off the bus and into the cool, rainy night. He walked away as the bus idled loudly on the side of the road.

Erik stopped on the corner and looked both ways. No cars raced by. The streets were clean in this area of town, even though the sidewalks were cracked. There was no trash littering the streets. No homeless people lying on the sidewalk, and no hookers on street corners, worn out from a life of sex for hire. The lights of businesses were off. The only real lights were the ones shining down from streetlamps. Erik looked back at the bus. It still sat where he got off. The interior lights were on, but the bus driver was nowhere to be seen.

"Hey," came the voice to his right. In the store window on the corner, showing through the display of female mannequins with no faces or hair and clothed in slick dresses, was the man in the bus window. He wore baggy jeans and a light coat and sneakers—the toe of the right one had a hole in it. He was soaked through from the rain, and his long hair clung to his skull.

"What do you want?"

"Just saying hey."

Erik went to the window. He touched the glass. The image did the same thing. "I've seen your face before."

"Oh, yes, you have. Quite often."

"Do I know you?"

The man smiled, looked toward the bus, then back at Erik. From off in the distance came sirens. "You might want to get a move on."

Erik nodded and left the image standing there. He didn't know if those sirens belonged to the police, but he had no plans of being around when they went by. When he reached the corner, he looked back. The image remained in the window, and the man stared at Erik with an intensity that uneased him. Erik shoved his hands into his jean pockets, hunched his shoulders, and crossed the street, leaving the man behind.

He didn't really know the area, but he thought he could find his way home easily enough. It took an hour or so, but he finally came upon familiar streets, these not as clean as the one where the bus dropped him off. Trash littered the broken sidewalks. The store fronts didn't hold glamourous looking mannequins, and many of the streetlights burned out years ago. Homeless people lay against walls with cardboard boxes for beds, pillows, and blankets, none of them dry. Hookers leaned against walls, none of them calling out to him for a good time tonight, baby. They knew Erik's type: poor. They wanted nothing to do with him.

"Spare some change so I can eat?"

The woman sat on the sidewalk, her back against the wall. She was as wet as everything else. Her heavy coat and knit hat did nothing against the constant downpour. One glove-covered hand extended up and out toward Erik. Though she was soaked through, her face was still dirty, her clothes soiled.

"I have no change," Erik said. He walked on.

"Nothing to spare for an old woman?"

He closed his eyes and stopped. He pinched the bridge of his nose with a finger and thumb. How many times did he have to say *no* to get the point across? He turned and looked back at the woman, at the grimy clothes, dirty face, and gray hair that peeked out from beneath the knit cap.

"Walk away, Erik," came the whisper in his left ear.

"No," came the whisper from the right. That voice was stronger and sounded vaguely familiar. He turned around to see no one there, but someone was. He was as sure of that as he was the rain pouring down on him right then.

"I know you," Erik said.

He turned back to the woman. Her hand was no longer out, and she leaned to the side against the wall. Her eyes were closed, and her mouth slightly open. Erik frowned. He rubbed his face with both hands, closed his eyes tight for several seconds, then opened them. The woman now leaned further, her side almost touching the ground. Her hand lay limp beside her. He shook his head and backed away from the woman.

"I'm hearing things."

"Are you?" came that familiar whisper.

Erik looked around. Again, he saw no one but was certain someone was there with him. He ran a hand through his hair and went up the road. At first, he walked slower than he had, his eyes searching the shadows along the buildings for anyone. He picked up his pace to a quick walk, hoping to get away from the voice, the person stalking him in the shadows. A block further and he was in a light jog, then running until he was full-out sprinting.

Erik almost missed the entrance to his basement level apartment, slid on the wet concrete and almost pitched head-first toward the ground when he tried to stop. He righted himself and looked around again. The world was dark, and the rain had slowed to a light drizzle. The patter of water on a steel awning across the street was a steady rat-a-tat-tat. No streetlights lit the area, casting the street in a thick, wet gray that dripped malice.

Erik's heart beat hard. His breaths came in sharp, steady rasps; his chest heaved, in and out, in and out. He licked his lips and made his way down the dozen steps, holding to the steel handrail with its flaking black paint. At the bottom of the steps, he slipped a tarnished brass key from one pocket and put it in the lock. A moment later, he was in the door and it was closed, and bolted for good measure.

He took a deep breath through his nose and released it through his mouth. His chest deflated, and a sudden feeling of stupidity swept over him. The man in the bus and store windows had been him. The conversation had been an exaggeration of his mind. Erik giggled. It was nothing more than one or two *ha*'s, but it was followed by a couple more. Before he could contain it, he was laughing hysterically at how silly he had been. Running from nothing like a man with his hair on fire, almost falling when he tried to stop outside his apartment, the way he slammed the door shut, afraid someone would follow him inside.

Erik shook his head. "Idiot." He pushed himself off the door and licked his lips. He wiped a hand across his mouth. A drink would be good right about then, but he was certain there were no beers in the dorm refrigerator he had, and there was certainly no whiskey anywhere in the apartment. Part of the rehabilitation deal was no alcohol of any kind, but beer wasn't really alcohol. Not in his mind, at least. Whiskey . . . whiskey was real alcohol, and that's what he wanted.

"You'll get in trouble," he whispered.

To his right, he heard the familiar voice whisper back, "You're already in trouble."

Erik frowned. "No, I'm not."

"Sure you are."

"Shut up. I'm not." Erik grabbed his ears, pulling the hair around them. He shut his eyes as tight as he could.

Another giggle came, this time from the voice. Then it grew silent.

Erik waited a minute, then two before pushing himself off the door and walking across the room. A threadbare recliner with a broken footrest sat in front of an old television that sat on a sagging wooden table. The television had seen better days but still had a screen that worked, even if a line ran down the right side of it, obscuring the picture a little in green, blue, and yellow.

The rest of the apartment was small. A kitchen sat off to his right, with that dorm sized refrigerator along with a stove and counter. The hall was nothing more than a square with four doorways: living room, bathroom, and two bedrooms. The bathroom was off to the left, one bedroom directly ahead of him, and the second one to his right. Erik frowned at this. Slamming the door should have brought his room-mate out of his room with an angry, "What's all the racket?"

Erik stood by the recliner looking toward the hall and waiting for Jim to burst from his room in stained underwear and no shirt, gray hair wild on his head and wilder on his chest. He wasn't a thin man, but he was tall and carried his bulk well while wearing clothes. Without clothes . . . he wasn't a pretty sight. After a couple of minutes and no raging Jim, he relaxed, let out a breath, and licked his lips.

The only perk to the apartment was free cable, even if it was only nineteen channels and nothing premium. He couldn't order movies of any rating, G to X, didn't matter. Erik didn't care much for movies.

He sat in the recliner. It tilted to his left a little but didn't tip over. The remote sat between the armrest and the lumpy seat cushion. He grabbed it, hit the power button, and waited several seconds as the television came to life, first lighting up white, dimming to gray before a hazy black and white picture began to form. He only turned the television on to block out any noises coming from the street or the apartment above him, tuned it to the one local channel it truly picked up. The image of a woman standing in front of a car in a dress took shape and eventually went from black and white to an entirely too bright screen with its green, blue, and yellow streak running along the right side. The woman spoke of car insurance like it was something everyone could afford. Erik knew better. His car insurance was the monster SR-22 variety, and almost twelve hundred bucks a month wasn't affordable. When the next commercial came on, Erik closed his eyes. In seconds, he was asleep.

And Erik dreamed.

He stood inside a mirror, looking out onto the bathroom of his apartment. The bathtub was stained brown and red, the toilet seat hung on by one loose plastic bolt, there was no lid. The sink below the mirror he looked out of had small hairs on the sides and in the basin, left behind after he shaved. Splotches of blood had dried on the floor around the sink. The mirror itself was filmy with condensation spots left behind from semi-warm showers. Along with those spots were pink smudges that obscured some of the scenery in front of him.

Erik turned and looked at the same scene behind him. The 2-D world he was trapped in held sharp points at every angle. The brown and red stains in the tub and floor and along the sink basin were brighter and somehow still wet.

When he looked back in the mirror, the bus stop had replaced his bathroom. The man who had been sitting beside him was still there, his hands between his legs, his jaw now slack, eyes still closed. A dark spot appeared on his left side and spread to the bench. He looked up. A giggle escaped him as a smile tried to spread across his face.

"What the . . ."

He closed his eyes and shook his head. He licked his lips and opened his eyes. The inside of the bus appeared, the driver laying on the floor halfway between the front and center doors. A halo of red crowned his head and the floor beneath him.

"Wake up!" Erik yelled and tapped the glass with one knuckle. "Wake up!"

The bus driver lifted his head from the floor and looked toward Erik. Blood spilled from a hole in his throat. He smiled. He was missing a tooth on the bottom row. He giggled, then broke into a full laugh.

"This isn't happening. This isn't . . ."

Erik took a step back, his hands out in front of him. His legs hit the edge of the bathtub, and he almost tipped over into it. He caught himself and stood straight again. In the mirror was a dark street. A woman lay on her side on the ground, her back to a rundown building. Her nose was swollen, and her mouth open. Her face was a shade of blue verging on purple. The woman didn't move or open her eyes, but a laugh came from her open mouth.

"No. This isn't happening."

Erik swung a closed fist at the mirror.

He woke. His eyes snapped open. His body jerked to his left. The recliner teetered for a couple of seconds before tipping over altogether and dumping Erik onto the floor. Sand and dirt clung to his sweaty face, and a chill formed over his body. He pushed himself up, then stood. He didn't bother righting the recliner. His head hurt, and he was only vaguely aware the television was still on, its screen a glowing white and blue light in the otherwise dark room.

The eight a.m. news was on. The man behind the news desk was dressed in a yellow shirt and a slightly off-colored blue tie. A part ran down one side of his dark hair. Next to him was a young woman with brown hair and in an emerald-green dress. She was attractive and clearly there as eye candy to help the show's ratings.

"In local news," the man started, "a man was found slain early this morning in the bus he drove for City Transit. Sometime between ten and eleven last night, Howard Reely was stabbed to death on his bus. His body was found by police after receiving a report that the bus had been sitting in one spot with its doors open for a couple of hours. Police entered the bus and found Reely lying face down near the front of the bus . . ."

A giggle escaped Erik. He clamped his hands over his mouth.

"So much murder in this town," came a whisper to his right.

He turned, expecting to see Jim, but no one was there.

The news anchor continued into another story. "In what police are saying could be related to the death of Reely, a homeless man was found dead on a bus stop bench this morning. Like Reely, he had been stabbed to death . . ."

Another giggle came. "Two people in one night?"

"All these murders . . ."

Erik looked around, spun in a circle. "Where are you? I know you're here. Where are you?"

A laugh was followed by, "I'm right here."

"Where?" The beating of his heart picked up. The sweat on his body had cooled, and the chill that swept over him sent shivers up and down his arms and back.

"Come on, Erik. You know where I am."

"No. No, I don't. Where are you? *Who* are you?"

Erik crouched down behind the tipped-over recliner, his hands holding on to the armrest tight enough to make his knuckles white. He looked from side to side, searching in the glow of the television for anyone who could be in there with him.

"A homeless woman was found dead on the sidewalk on the East side of town this morning . . ."

Erik barely heard the news anchor, but another laugh came from deep within him, this one more than a giggle and verging on unhinged.

". . . stabbed to death . . ."

Erik grabbed his ears and squeezed. He fell backward onto his bottom and pulled his knees to his chest. For several minutes, he rocked back and forth, his tongue darting out to lick his rapidly chapping lips.

The laughter grew louder.

"Stop laughing," Erik yelled. "Stop laughing!"

The laughter ebbed to a giggle, then an occasional "ha" before growing quiet.

"So much murder in this town. So much murder in this town. So much murder in this town," Erik mumbled.

At some point, he stood. His heart still beat too hard for his liking. His skin was still cold, and the chills made him shake almost violently.

"Wash your face, Erik," he whispered.

The bathroom light was a harsh yellow compared to the glow of the television. The yellow painted walls amplified the brightness. The mirror was stained with condensation and pimple puss. The toilet seat was broken, with half of it on the floor. The water in the bowl was an ugly beer color. A ring of brown circled the edges of the water. There was no shower curtain, and the shower head had been broken off at some point. The tub itself was no longer white but stained brown and . . .

Erik screamed. He backed away from the tub and bumped against the door he had closed at some point. Jim lay in the tub in his not-so-white underwear, the front stained yellow.

His considerable gut held so many stab wounds. One finger lay on the floor between the tub and the toilet.

Laughter came from the mirror. Erik's face held a confused shock to it, but the reflection was all teeth and gaps and closed-eyed laughter.

"Stop laughing!" Erik swung his hand as hard as he could. The mirror shattered. Pieces of reflective glass dug into his palm, slicing it open. Other pieces landed in the sink or the floor with the tinkling sound of breaking glass.

Erik's bottom lip shook as pain raced through his palm and into his wrist. Bright red blood spilled from the myriad of wounds and dripped to the floor. He stared at his hand, his brain mesmerized by the pooling blood in his palm. When he laughed this time, it was completely him and not a psychological carbon copy. He backed into the door again, the laughter squeezing out every breath his lungs could muster. He slid down until his bottom touched the floor. A deep breath was only a momentary reprieve for his starving lungs. More laughter followed, and tears spilled from his eyes and down his reddening cheeks. His head grew light.

A minute passed, then a second and third one as he tried to regain his breath. Finally, the laughter subsided enough to push the lightheaded feeling away and allow his lungs to fill with air.

Even after composing himself, his face was stuck in a humorless grin, the muscles aching and tense. Though his head hurt and his hand screamed from the open cuts the mirror made, he didn't grimace or cry or try to stop the bleeding. Instead, he picked up a triangular piece of mirror. In it was a jagged image of himself.

"I know you," he whispered, his frozen smile not wavering. His reflection didn't respond. "I've always known you."

The image still didn't respond. It only looked back at him, silly smile and all.

"I'm you," Erik said. "And you're me. You . . . you killed all those people. That bus driver. That homeless guy. That woman on the sidewalk asking for change. You killed Jim. And you know what? You liked it. I know you did."

Erik let out another giggle, then licked his lips. "All these murders . . . these murders in this town . . . you . . . you did them. And you liked it. I . . . I liked it. We liked it." He shook his head, but his eyes never left the sliver of mirror in his good hand.

Without thinking, Erik drove the glass into his wrist and ran it all the way up to the crook in his elbow. Skin flayed open, and blood rushed from the deep wound. As his life began flowing from him and his world grew dim, Erik laughed until even that subsided to a giggle, then a *ha*.

From the many broken pieces of mirror came one question, echoed loudly in his ears from a million versions of himself. "What's one more murder?"

Erik laughed.

IRINA GAIDAMACHUK

"MY HUSBAND WOULDN'T GIVE ME MONEY FOR VODKA."

—IRINA GAIDAMACHUK

KILL HYMN
BY LISA VASQUEZ

THE BOYS' CHOIR SANG FROM THE BALCONY, THEIR SOFT voices rising through the thick smoke of incense. Father Carter sat hunched in the front pew, his blank stare focused on the flickering candlelight. The walls were covered with scenes of crackled fresco figures, an army of angels and cherubs blurring in and out of focus, their serene faces mocking the turbulence inside him.

Sister Natalie walked past him as quiet as a mouse. Her worn leather shoes with thick soles absorbed all sound across the marble floor until she came to a stop. In front of her was a statue of Mary cradling her infant son, born of the most revered holy mother. It was a tender icon compared to the statue at the opposite end of St Michael Church, where the same mother now stared down at the battered and bloodied Christ who was splayed across her lap.

Father Carter let out a slow exhale and bowed his head, making the sign of the cross. Sister Natalie placed fresh flowers in an empty vase, then turned and offered him a smile. Her faded, kind blue eyes were framed by wrinkles formed through 40 years of devoted service and countless tears for the sick and poor for whom she lived to serve.

He smiled back. It was a small, practiced smile, more like a smirk.

Looking down at his hands, his eyes settled on the crucifix entangled between his fingers where the small, silver cross rested against his palm. It stared up at him from the embedded mark it left in his skin from squeezing it too tight.

He was a mask of peacefulness on the outside, but inside, a storm was rumbling at the edges of his soul. His hands trembled. Cold beads of sweat lined his brow, threatening to betray the façade of a calm exterior. Beyond it, he hid a dark secret. The halls of his mind echoed with loud whispers where the shadow watched and reveled at his suffering.

Dear God, he thought. *Why does my soul feel on fire? Why does it feel like I carry Hell within my heart?*

Paul Carter the man versus Father Carter was a war of duality fought on the silent battlefield of his mind. Once a bright-eyed seminarian eager to serve, he was now an acolyte of a dark entity. *It* resided among his once unblemished faith, threatening to snuff out his light. The entity was growing every day, feeding on his guilt and self-loathing. Equal sides pulling against one another until he thought it might *actually* split him in two.

No amount of prayer could stop the shadow who lingered inside. A vile, relentless force, it was like thick tar attached to his internal organs, poisoning his blood until the inevitable took place. He would *become* the monster he struggled to restrain with nothing more than a frayed, unraveling leash.

The torment was enough to make him scream.

A hymn of lamentations to fill the church, he thought. *Each note a cacophony of conflicting desires. Every chord striking a nerve, amplifying my sense of futility. The shadow at the helm, conducting a Psalm containing my confessions. These primal urges masked by my exterior of a pious devout man. A fucking constant reminder I'm a broken meat puppet dangling on entrails, forced to dance to the beat of the devil's banjo, its blackened fingers manipulating the strings, forcing me to skip over the open flame.*

He lowered his head in shame.

The festering madness rose inside him again. He kissed the cross, clutching it against his palm once again, then stood. He liked the pain.

He *deserved* the pain.

His knees tingled from hours of useless prayer. He wrapped the beads of his rosary around his wrist tighter like a garrote until he could feel it cut off the circulation to his sinful hands.

The heat of his guilt pricked his skin, sweat seeping into the open wounds of his back where his shirt stuck to him. Hot, red flog marks sticky with dots of blood wept from bruised mortal flesh.

"Amen," he whispered through clenched teeth.

He took in a slow, deep breath. The Shadow was laughing in his ear.

"*Go,*" It said with a hiss, as if the incense could reach out from the censor sitting on top the altar to whisper to him. "*Go see her again. We crave her.*"

"Please," Father Carter pleaded under his breath.

There were no secrets here. The priest lifted his gaze to meet the ever-watchful gazes positioned around him. The oversized eyes of the cherubs. The doe-like stare of the martyrs and saints. The disappointed, judgmental eyes of the crucified Christ.

I confess I am weak. Oh, Lord, why? Why do you abandon me to the darkness?

"*GO!*" It commanded.

Anger bled, hemorrhaged into his chest until he could taste sulfur on the back of his tongue.

His legs buckled. To keep his balance, he reached out to the pew beside him before going down to a knee, genuflecting before a God who no longer heard him. If it ever had.

The moment he felt the marble touch the bent joint, a growl filled the chambers of his mind, rattling the bars that held the Beast imprisoned. He could feel its claws rip and rend at the inside of his skull. He gritted his teeth, grinding the tooth enamel until he heard cracking.

I can't do this anymore, he thought to himself. The weight of his sin bore down on him. It threatened to break his back as he resisted the force of gravity pushing his face to the floor. The Beast hissed in resentment to the act of submission. *It* paced like a caged animal, pulling at the chains of restraint.

The sweat in Father Carter's hairline clung to his dark curls until they matted against his skin. Salt and oil wept from his pores, and he stood yet again. Control was an illusion slipping into the porcelain bowl of a gas station bathroom. No matter how many times you flushed to get the water clean, something always floated back up.

The Beast cackled like a lunatic. *Its* hoarse laughter sounded like something coming from emphysemic lungs, popping and bubbling through thick, green phlegm. *It* breathed out, releasing a miasma of air that reeked of sick death and clung to the air like nicotine.

Father Paul took in a deep breath against the suffocating burden of carrying another being inside. He had to go to her. It was the only way. *She* was the only salvation. Not the man draped across the wooden cross. Not the imaginary spirit in the sky he prayed to every single day for release. Not the magic wine in his polished cup. Not the stale wafers that clung to the inside of his mouth, gagging him with his own truth.

Not God.

It was *her*.

"Magdelena."

His whispered her name under his breath, and still, it carried on the acoustics of the church walls. It slapped every martyr and saint with its invisible hand until it reached the army of angels staring down from the painted clouds. He could almost envision their robes fluttering in the breeze created by her name floating past them.

Bile rose into his throat. It tasted like shit from his gurgling bowels. He took his handkerchief out of his robe pocket and swiped it on his moist upper lip. When he looked down at the starched white fabric, he could see the smear of his jaundiced skin like the Shroud of Turin.

One foot in front of the other, he trudged through the fragrant nave, his back to the pulpit where he had spoken hours before—a false prophet of the scriptures he no longer believed in.

He approached an older woman on her knees, her rosary wrapped around her wrists and snaked through her fingers like shackles. She was praying so hard he thought he could hear her thoughts through her paper-thin skin. She wasn't long for the world, but she was here, confessing her sins. Begging for forgiveness on the chance she might get a ticket through the Pearly Gates.

When Father Carter was close enough, she reached out with an arthritic, gnarled hand to clutch at the hem of his robe. Before he could protest, she brought it to her lips and kissed the black cloth, then let it fall back to the floor, draping over the tips of his shoes.

"Pray for me, Father," she said, lifting her eyes to him. The color in them had long ago faded. Like life slipping away from her. Though they were clouded with glaucoma and half blind, she sought out his blessings and prayers.

The priest reached out and pressed his hand to the top of

her head. She leaned into it, letting tears spill from the corners of her eyes. Waiting.

Waiting to hear the words that would open the doors of heaven when she passed from this world to the next. She would not make it to the morning. He could feel it. The Beast could feel it. *It* purred beneath his skin. He felt the ripples of the vibration through his veins like tendrils, through his arm, to his wrist, and into his fingers.

The old woman's eyes widened, and he witnessed the moment when she realized *something* was off about him.

"There is no God here today," Father Carter whispered down to her. When her mouth fell open and her face twisted with shock and despair, he pressed closer. He listened week after week to her placating confessions. He listened to the cries of her children, who she abused for years. He took note of the mistreatment of her husband, who died working his fingers to the bone so she could spend every penny. Not on the children. Not on the neglected home. She squandered the money on her designer dresses and high-end jewelry.

"When you die, you'll be nothing more than a sack of deformed, brittle bones in a cheap box. Your children will toss you into the dirt and forget you like a used snot rag. You can pray, and pray, and pray, but you know what you did. You *know*."

Cocking his arm back, he shoved the old woman by her face and watched her fall onto the floor with a gasp followed by a yelp. The impact dislocated her arm and forced the wind from her lungs.

There was no more remorse. *It was in charge.*

"Magdelena," it hissed, now finding his vocal cords. *It* was growing stronger. The Beast slid his skin on like a skin suit and flexed its talons into his finger gloves. *It* was warm and comfortable wrapped in his flesh. Father Carter could feel the Beast's eyes push up behind his, the pressure making jabbing, knife-like pain clusters bloom into view. He could see brilliant flashes of color and light like high beams from oncoming traffic.

One step in front of the other, it walked him to the basement stairs. He flicked the light switch to his left, then took a step forward. The single bulb hanging above rolled off his head and swayed back and forth, flickering.

Please, he begged. *I don't want to go down there again.*

The Beast only laughed in response. *It* would punish him again for disobeying. It would make him pay with hours of unbearable pain. Father Carter no longer cared if *It* did. He knew this was the end for him.

Forcing through an unseen force, he exerted his will to retake control of his body. When he could feel his limbs again, he thrust his arms out to either side, jamming the heels of his palms against the wall.

He grew dizzy and sick with vertigo as he stared down into the darkness. The smell of the basement rose until it filled his nostrils with the putrid mixture of mold, death, and sickening sweet incense.

"No!" he shouted.

His voice reverberated off the walls and ricocheted back so hard it was like a physical punch to his temple.

He could feel warm, wet liquid trickling from his nose. It made a trail through the dewdrops of sweat until it settled in the crevice where his two lips met. The copper taste of blood seeped in until it met the tip of his tongue.

"Stop . . . Please, stop! I cannot take any . . . more," he cried out. The words broke into a helpless whimper, knowing *It* would win. *It* always won.

The ringing in his ears grew louder. Two hot pokers pressing in, in stereo. High-pitched speaker feedback sliced through his brain. He coughed, and blood sprayed from his mouth, minuscule droplets freckling the dingy, pale-blue walls.

The muscles of Father Carter's shoulders ached and quivered. Unwilling to give up until he was depleted of energy, he ground his molars together and squeezed his eyes shut, forcing unshed tears out onto his cheeks.

"Almighty God! Help me!"

"God is not here," the Beast croaked, its wretched voice like an old, heavy metal door closing in on him, locking him in the cellar of the church. *"You will never be free,"* It said. *"You are mine. You are herssss. Allllways."*

Distant memories replayed in his mind. The Beast was reminding him of his recent iniquity.

A dark-haired woman beneath him. The two breathing each other in. Naked flesh, clinging sheets. Her moans mixed with blasphemous cries and sinful expressions. He had never heard such things before.

He pushed his mouth against hers to silence her. To taste her. But she continued to undulate beneath him like a serpent, there to tempt his faith.

In the half-light of the candles lit for loved ones' souls, a symbol of prayers filling the darkness of suffering, he lifted her into his arms, then pushed her against the wall, crushing her with his weight. The rougher he was, the more vile her salacious pleas and writhing became.

He stared down at her neck and watched as it vibrated with her purrs of pleasure, her body jolting with every thrust of him inside of her. Her almond-shaped gaze stared up at him in reverence. Father Carter put his hand around her throat, and her eyes grew wide with surprise.

There was laughing now. He could hear it as he continued to give in to the sins of the flesh. Over his shoulder, a chittering of tiny laughter as if the painted cherubs came to life to judge him. Judge his performance. Judge his lack of decorum.

This is the house of God . . .

God is not here today.

What willpower he had left melted away with a sob. The priest's hands fell to his sides, and his chin dropped to his chest.

Helpless, he thought to himself.

"*Weak,*" the Beast hissed. "*Worthless waste of space. You stand at the pulpit with your pretty dress, your big book of lies, and spew shit from your lips. The lips used for Magdalenaaaa. Slave, to Mag . . . Da . . . Lenaaaa.*"

Shut up!

"*Go to her!*"

I can't!

"*You willll . . .*"

Lifting his hands to his ears, Father Carter crushed his palms to his ears like a vice, squeezing his skull as hard as he could to keep what little sanity was left, inside. To keep *its* voice out. When he pulled his hands away, he brought them to eye level. They were soaked in blood and sweat.

"If I go down there," he sniveled, "I will die."

The hoarse laughter in his brain mocked him. He was fighting for his life. Going down there, going to *her* would result in his death.

"Will it hurt?"

The words were feeble as they came out of him, full of fear and desperation.

"*Yessssss,*" it whispered.

The priest curled into himself as if he had been kicked in his stomach. His bowels gurgled, accompanying the lightning strike of pain. Sinking down to the step, Father Carter felt his legs go numb. Taking a breath was hard. Reaching for his rosary, he clutched it until the wooden cross almost snapped.

"He's not here." The Beast's voice slithered through his ear holes and down his spine.

Ignoring the voice, Father Carter pursed his lips together and pressed the crucifix to his forehead while he prayed. It was all he had left before life was ripped from him.

Whatever was on the other side, he would grasp for it with both hands.

"Oh, Lord," he began. His bowels churned like an angry volcano, heat searing him from the inside out. "Oh! Dear Father in Heaven! Forgive your poor, wretched servant."

The pain inside of him was unbearable now. Through the screeching tinnitus and the drumming of his heartbeat in his ears, a voice called to him.

"Magdalena," he whispered, raising his eyes. White light closed in, a vignette halo framing his sight and creating a tunnel. "I need you."

Running low on strength, Father Carter slid down one step, then another. Then another. He continued to drag himself down each one until he was able to reach the bottom. Behind him, a red and black ribbon of shit and blood trailed in his wake.

The world spun out of focus, but all he could think about was getting to Magdalena. If he could just hold her one more time, all of this would go away.

The nights he hid in plain clothes in the seedy bars to be with her, the lies he told for showing up late and disheveled to morning mass, and the reason he gave up his eternal soul. All of it was for her.

The Beast pressed its finger to the back of his neck, the familiar itch; a nail scratching the soft tissue in the back of his throat, slithering down into his belly before plunging into the cesspool of his stomach. Ulcers flared, their wounds gaping wide like small, hungry birds waiting for their next meal. They festered and pussed, leaking infection into his gut.

His clammy hands reached out in front of him, where a blackened hoof appeared, blocking him from his love.

"Will you die for her?" it asked with an amused curiosity. *"Or will you die for your Christ?"* It paused, allowing the question to drive home. *"Will you give Him back your soul? Or will you stay forever with her?"*

"Her," Father Carter whispered with a strain, knowing it may be his last word. Yes, her. She was the first one; she'd be the last. She, who had never forsaken him, always loyal and forgiving.

With her, he was a man. With her, he felt alive. He could laugh and forget the bitterness of the world, the vile confessions of the parishioners who wore duality of sinner and saint . . . The lies. All of the god damned lies . . . They were washed away by her.

Father Carter pushed the Beast's hoof aside and crawled past it, reddish-pink dribble hanging from his nose and mouth as he moved forward. When he got to the cellar door across the room, he was panting with exertion. He raised his head and looked upon the crucifix hanging from the center like a knocker and began to laugh.

The sound of his lungs whistled like a pair of deflated balloons; the oxygen seeping past his fattening tongue turned into silent sobs.

"God," he forced out from behind blue lips. Breathing was becoming laborious. "God is not here . . . today."

He pushed his hand against the door, and the light from the cellar shone into the small closet of miscellaneous office supplies. Dragging himself forward, he reached the drawer of an old metal desk stashed away in the corner. He rummaged inside until his fingers caressed the curved glass bottle.

When he pulled it out, he propped himself against the wall and cradled it to his chest. He made it. He was reunited with her once again. He looked down at the label and let his thumb brush across it with affection.

Magdelena was written in bold letters against the yellow background. The priest unscrewed the cap and brought the bottle to his lips. The smell of the alcohol filled every bit of his being. He tipped it back and took several deep swallows until the burn was too much. The last gulp caused him to sputter. Rum and blood splashed onto the front of his robes until he choked.

Blood oozed out of every orifice, staining the concrete beneath him with a mixture of liquor and feces. The sepsis of his necrotic bowel had poisoned his blood. Years of drinking finally caught up to him, and he died with his true love wrapped in his embrace.

www.ingramcontent.com/pod-product-compliance
Lightning Source LLC
Chambersburg PA
CBHW071440260626

47170CB00008B/2780